BOOK 2

**ONCE AGAIN FOR NIKO** — E.S.F.
Special thanks to Kelli C. for terrific editing; to Jared, the best marine
mechanic ever; to Chelsea, Steve T., MW, and everyone at the East Hampton Library.

**FOR MOM — MAY THE WIND ALWAYS FILL YOUR SAILS.**
**FOR STEPHANIE — YOU ARE MY ANCHOR AND MY LIGHTHOUSE.** — J.B.

First Chronicle Books LLC paperback edition, published in 2015.
Originally published in hardcover in 2014 by Chronicle Books LLC.

ISBN 978-1-4521-2875-7

The Library of Congress has cataloged the original edition as follows:

Farber, Erica.
  Operation Fireball / by E.S. Farber ; illustrated by Jason Beene.
    p. cm. — (Fish Finelli ; bk. 2)
  Summary: Fish Finelli and his friends are fixing up their boat, the Fireball, for the Captain
Kidd Classic race, and more than anything Fish wants to beat Bryce, the local bully, but a local
girl named Clementine is complicating his plans for the race.
  ISBN 978-1-4521-1083-7 (alk. paper)
  1. Motorboat racing—Juvenile fiction. 2. Motorboats—Juvenile fiction. 3. Bullying—Juvenile
fiction. 4. Friendship—Juvenile fiction. [1. Racing—Fiction 2. Motorboats—Fiction. 3. Bul-
lies—Fiction. 4. Friendship—Fiction.] I. Beene, Jason, ill. II. Title.

PZ7.F22275Ope 2014
813.6—dc23

                              2013003263

Manufactured in China.

Interior design by Amy Achaibou and Lauren Michelle Smith.
Cover design by Lauren Michelle Smith.
Typeset in Century Schoolbook.
The illustrations in this book were rendered digitally.

10 9 8 7 6 5 4 3 2 1

The name Seagull is a registered trademark of John Freeman (Sales) Ltd.

Chronicle Books LLC
680 Second Street
San Francisco, CA 94107

Chronicle Books—we see things differently.
Become part of our community at www.chroniclekids.com.

## OPERATION FIREBALL

### BY E.S. FARBER • ILLUSTRATED BY JASON BEENE

chronicle books · san francisco

# 10,000 WAYS THAT
# WON'T WORK

"On the count of three," I said. "One . . . two . . ."

"Two and a half," said Roger, grinning so his brown eyes crinkled at the corners.

"Two and three-quarters," said T. J.

"Three!" We picked up the Seagull motor and slid it into the drum of water.

SWOOSH!

Water spilled all over us and all over the driveway.

"Guys, that is way too much water," I said.

"It wasn't too much water *before* the motor went in," said T. J.

"I know," I said. "It's the Archimedes Principle. The volume of the motor will displace an amount of water equal to the—"

"Sheesh, Fish," said Roger. "We've done the bucket test six times already this afternoon. We could have been shooting hoops with Two O or paddleboarding, but no, we're in your driveway—"

"One more time. It's going to work. I just know it," I said, crossing my fingers behind my back so Roger couldn't see.

After we emptied out some water, we lowered the Seagull motor into the drum until the propeller was submerged.

The Seagull is an awesome motorboat engine. Roger, T. J., and I bought it with the money we got for finding Captain Kidd's treasure. That's right—we found Captain Kidd's treasure. It's a long story, but no, it wasn't gold and jewels. It was a bunch of old papers, a busted-up silver teapot, and some long underwear. Weird, right? Who would have thought pirates wore long underwear?

I pulled a basin wrench out of my tool belt and bolted the motor to the side of the drum.

"How are you boys doing?" called Uncle Norman, sticking his head out the window. He was fixing the kitchen sink and keeping an eye on us while my mom and dad went grocery shopping.

"Good!" I called back.

"Good and wet!" Roger grinned.

"Wet's okay," said Uncle Norman. "Just be careful."

"All set." I handed Roger the manual as Uncle Norman disappeared back inside. Uncle Norman is the best uncle ever. He taught me most of what I know about motors, because he has a boat. He also gave me my nickname, Fish. My real name is Norman, after him. One day I was on his boat when a bluefish took a chomp out of his finger. I laughed and said, "Fish." It was my first word, and it's been my name ever since.

Roger cleared his throat. "And now, ladies and gentlemen, or should I say, gentleman and gentleman, for the—"

"Will you just read the instructions?" I said.

"Chillax, Fish. Ah, where was I?" Roger stared blankly at the instructions.

"Fuel tap?" said T. J. helpfully.

"Open," I said, pulling the fuel tap.

"Choke?" said T. J., chewing on a mouthful of candy corn.

"Closed," I said.

"Press the tickler on the carburetor," T. J. said.

I opened the carb until a little fuel spilled out.

"Open the throttle to full," added T. J. "Oh, and make sure the motor is in neutral."

"Wow!" Roger looked up from the manual. "How did you know that, T. J.?"

T. J. shrugged. "Simple. It's like making the Super Sundae Special at Toot Sweets. First goes the hot fudge, then the gummy worms, then the ice cream. Next is the strawberry syrup and marshmallows. Then whipped cream, Sno-Caps, and sprinkles go on top."

I shook my head. T. J. is like a piñata. You never know what's going to come out of his mouth, the same way you never know what's going to come out of a piñata.

I wrapped the pull cord clockwise three times around the rope pull. "Ready, guys?" I said, steadying the tank with my left hand.

"Wait!" Roger ran into the garage.

RAT-TAT-TAT! RAT-TAT-TAT!

"What Operation Fireball needs is a drumroll." Roger banged a hammer against an old cookie tin with a reindeer on it.

The *Fireball* is the name of our boat. It's a whaler from the 1970s that the three of us have been fixing up. We're going to enter it in the Captain Kidd Classic, the biggest boat race of the summer. We're also planning to beat snooty Bryce Billings in the race, so Operation Fireball is our secret code name.

Roger and T. J.'s eyes were on me as I turned the flywheel clockwise. I had done every little thing the manual said. This time I was positive I did it right. I took a deep breath and gave a sharp pull on the rope.

Nothing.

I pulled a little harder.

Nothing.

I wrapped the cord again. Then I pulled on the rope.

Still nothing.

"Tartar sauce!" I kicked a rock in frustration. It ricocheted off the oil drum and hit me. "Ow!" I rubbed my knee.

"Another failure," said Roger, beating a slow RAT-TAT-TAT.

Roger was right. I had failed—again. All of a sudden, I remembered something Thomas Edison said before he invented the phonograph (the very first machine that could record sound and play it back).

"I have not failed," I said. "I've just found ten thousand ways that won't work."

## THOMAS EDISON (1847–1931)

In 1877, inventor Thomas Edison was working on the telegraph when he noticed that the noise the paper tape made when played at high speed through the machine sounded like spoken words. Edison took a tinfoil cylinder and a needle and made the first phonograph that could record sound. The outside horn phonograph was produced from approximately 1898–1931. And you know the first words he ever recorded? "Mary had a little lamb!"

Roger and T. J. both looked at me.

"You've got to be kidding me, Fish!" Roger said. "You are not really thinking we are going to do the bucket test nine thousand, nine hundred, and ninety-three more times."

He and T. J. groaned.

"Don't worry," I said. "I have a plan." I didn't quite yet, but I was sure I would think of something any minute.

Suddenly, there was a piercing scream. AAAAHHHHH!!!

# CHAMPION TEETER-TOTTER OF BLAH-BU-DE-BLAH

Roger, T. J., and I raced to my backyard. My little sister, Feenie, and Mmm, T. J.'s little sister, were staring at the bushes between my house and Roger's house. They both wore sparkly fairy wings, as usual. There was a baby carriage turned over on the grass, along with a baby blanket and a bottle.

"What's up, ladies?" asked Roger.

"It's Tatiana!" said Mmm.

"She jumped out of the carriage. We were saving her from—oops!" Feenie clapped her hand over her mouth.

"Saving her from what, Fee?" I asked. Feenie had the same guilty look on her face she got whenever she pretended some teeny piece of brownie *was so* my equal half.

"Nothing," said Feenie, shaking her head so her pigtails bobbed up and down.

"Tatiana ran away," said Mmm.

"What?!" T. J. said, his face so white that all of his freckles stood out.

Roger and I looked at each other in surprise. T. J. never got upset, not even the time he got the mini G. I. Joe rifle stuck up his nose and had to go to the emergency room to have it taken out.

"Margaret Mary Mahoney," he said, using Mmm's real, full name, which no one ever called her. "What did you do with Champion Tatiana of Britney Belle?"

Mmm just glared at T. J., her blue eyes narrowed into angry slits.

"Oh, boy. Mom is going to be so mad." He popped an entire handful of candy corn in his mouth and started crunching like crazy.

Mmm started crying. "Don't worry, Mmm." Feenie put an arm around her. "We will find her. We're Fapits. We have magic powers."

In case you're wondering, a Fapit is a Fairy Princess in Training.

"Who, may I ask, is Champion Teeter-Totter of Blah-Bu-De-Blah?" said Roger.

"The most valuable kitten in Britney Belle's litter," said T. J. "You know how my mom breeds cats and shows them in cat shows? Well, Tatiana won the Cat Fancy Show twice, which makes her a double champion. Some lady wants to buy her for a bunch of money. My mom's going to blow her top if we don't find her. That cat is worth over a thousand dollars."

"Whoa!"

Out of the corner of my eye, I caught a movement in the hedge. A small black, white, and orange paw poked out. "Look."

"Tatiana!" screamed the girls.

"Champion Teeter-Totter of Blah-Bu-De-Blah!" said Roger. "After that cat on the double!"

Mmm and Feenie ran toward the hedge, their fairy wings flapping.

"Don't!" said T. J. "You're going to scare Champion Tatiana away."

Too late. The cat raced toward the front yard in a blur of orange, black, white, and pink. Everyone ran after her.

"What's that pink thing on her head?" T. J. asked.

"A baby bonnet," said Mmm.

"So she would look like a baby, not a kitty cat," said Feenie.

Feenie and Mmm would make pretty good undercover operatives if they weren't only four-and-a-half years old.

We all looked around the yard.

"Champion Teeter-Totter of Blah-Bu-De-Blah, where are you?" asked Roger.

DIRECTIONAL MICROPHONE

NIGHT VISION GOGGLES

## UNDERCOVER

A secret agent or spy who is operating in the field—*under cover*—pretending to be someone who is not a spy in order to hide the fact that he or she is a spy.

T. J.'s stomach rumbled so loudly, we all jumped.

"How could you be hungry at a time like this?" I asked. "I thought you said it was a matter of life and death."

T. J. sighed. "Tater Tots."

"What do Tater Tots have to do with anything?"

"I know I'd stake my life on a platter of crunchy potato snacks," said Roger.

"Tater Tots are my favorite kind of potatoes," said T. J., as if that explained everything.

"Champion Teeter-Totter Tater Tot," said Roger. "Now there's a tongue twister."

"Tater Tots sounds like Teeter-Totter—" began T. J.

Just then there was a flash of pink behind the big pine tree at the end of my driveway.

"Tatiana!" said the girls.

Everyone ran down the driveway except for me. I headed to the garage to get my bike. We were going to need wheels if we wanted to catch this cat.

I tiptoed inside so my dog, Shrimp, who liked to sleep under the picnic table, wouldn't hear me. I started wheeling my bike out and was almost to the driveway when SQUEAK! Next thing I knew, Shrimp bounded toward me, jumped up, and nearly knocked me down. No one knew he was part Saint Bernard when we got him as a puppy.

WOOF!

"Shrimp! Stay!" I pointed to the house.

Shrimp tilted his head to one side.

"Stay, boy! This is a cat-rescue mission. You'll only get in the way."

WOOF! Shrimp wagged his tail.

"I know you want to help, but stay, Shrimp. Do you hear me?!"

I hopped on my bike and pedaled down the driveway. T. J. was bent over with his hand out. Was he trying to bait the cat with candy corn?

WOOF! WOOF!

The cat darted out from behind the tree.

I turned around. Shrimp was lumbering down the driveway.

"She's heading for the street!" said Roger.

"Tatiana!" said the girls. "Come back!"

T. J. hopped on his bike, popped on his helmet, and took off. I started to pedal after him.

"Wait for me!" called Roger, grabbing my skateboard from the side of the driveway.

I felt a tug on the back of my bike and almost tipped over. "What the—"

"Trust me, Fish," said Roger, gripping my bike as he balanced on my skateboard. He had Feenie's pink Cinderella helmet on his head. "It'll be faster this way."

We followed T. J. as he turned down Cinnamon Street. Shrimp bounded after us. WOOF! I could see a streak of pink and orange tearing through the weeds heading for Red Fox Lane, where T. J. and Mmm lived. Maybe Champion Tatiana was going home.

I had to stand up and pump hard on my pedals to keep up with T. J. as he made the right onto Red Fox. The sweat was dripping down my back. It felt as if Roger weighed five hundred pounds.

"WOO-HOO!" Roger called. "Cat chasing is fun!"

"For *you*," I said. "I'm doing all the work."

T. J. slowed as he got to the white picket fence in front of his house. Champion Tatiana kept right on going. She began to run even faster.

"There she goes!" said T. J.

I raced after T. J. as he made a left onto Edge Road. Shrimp was running between us. T. J. kept going on Edge, past Lily Lane and Dune Lane. Boy, this cat sure could run.

Suddenly, T. J. made a sharp right onto Thither Lane.

"Watch out, Fish!" Roger swung sideways as I made the turn.

I slowed and straightened out so he could regain his balance. "You are *so* riding me all the way home," I said, gasping for breath.

We continued south toward the ocean. We were in the heart of the Lanes. The big mansions with pools and tennis courts are hidden behind tall hedges and gates. Most of the people who live there are summer people. They live someplace else, like in the city, and just come here for the summer and weekends. There's one house that's so big, they call it the Hotel because it has twenty-five bedrooms and a bowling alley.

T. J. skidded to a stop halfway down the lane in front of a cobblestone driveway and a big white fence that had to be close to eight feet tall.

"What are we doing here, T. J.?" I asked, trying to catch my breath. Shrimp stood beside me, panting and drooling, too.

T. J. shoved a handful of barbecue potato chips in his mouth and pointed up. There on the high branch of an old oak tree that stuck out past the top of the fence was a small black, orange, and white cat. She had lost the baby bonnet along the way.

"Champion Teeter-Totter of Blah-Bu-De-Blah!" said Roger. "Fancy meeting you here, you Cat Fancy Double Champion."

"Now what?" I said, eyeing the distance from the branch to the ground. If the fence was eight feet high, the branch was another six inches or so, making it close to eight-and-a-half feet.

"How . . . *mumble* . . . getter?" asked T. J., his mouth full of chips.

"Simple," said Roger with a grin. "The powers of persuasion."

"Huh?" said T. J., shoving even more chips in his mouth.

"It's like how my mom sells houses," said Roger. "You figure out what your client wants and then just remind them it's what they want when they see it. For instance, if a couple is buying a starter ranch that they can add on to after the first kid—"

"Roger!" I said. "Will you cut to the chase?"

"Look, we all want the same thing—for Teeter-Totter to get down. So all we have to do is remind her that her wish is our wish. Then TA-DA, everyone's happy."

T. J.'s stomach rumbled as he stared worriedly up at Champion Tatiana.

"Cats don't usually listen to people, Rog," I said, thinking of Dude, our old black cat. "They're not like dogs who respect dominant humans as alpha dogs and—"

"Watch this," said Roger, looking up at the cat with a big grin on his face. "Champion Teeter-Totter of Blah-Bu-De-Blah, it's time to come down. You know you want to."

Champion Tatiana looked away from us.

"Listen to me, Champion T. It's all right. Just move your little paws." Roger motioned with his hand.

The cat didn't move an inch. She didn't even look at him.

"Oh, well." Roger shrugged. "Guess the powers of persuasion don't work on cats. My mom says they don't always work on people, either. But don't sweat it. I have a Plan B."

"What is it?" asked T. J.

"A ladder," said Roger, swiping a chip out of T. J.'s hand and crunching on it.

"Not only do we not have a ladder, even if we got one, we can't carry it on a bike," I said.

"Hmm," said Roger. "Good point. Give me a minute to come up with Plan C."

"There's only one thing we can do," I said. "Climb that tree."

Roger and T. J. looked at the fence and then up at the tree where Champion Tatiana was sitting. Then they turned to me. We all knew who would be doing the climbing.

"Think a human pyramid will give you enough boost?" asked Roger.

I shrugged. It was going to have to.

"Okay, Teej," said Roger, patting him on the back. "One, two, three—go!"

T. J. dropped to his knees by the fence and bent over with his hands on the ground.

"Now me," said Roger. "Roger Huckleton, Ace Cat Chaser, steps up to—"

"Just do it, Roger!" I said, giving him a push toward T. J.

"Hands off the merchandise," Roger said. He climbed on top of T. J. but slipped off.

"Teej, quit eating. I can't balance if you don't hold still."

T. J. swallowed hard. "I don't mean to eat. It just happens when I'm nervous."

Roger climbed up again and balanced on his knees on top of T. J. Then he put his hands down by T. J.'s shoulders.

"All right, guys, here I come."

This was the critical moment. Carefully, I put one foot on T. J.'s back and then another.

"Oomph!"

So far, so good.

"Ready, Rog?"

"All systems—go!"

I climbed knees first onto Roger's back.

"Finelli, you weigh a ton," said Roger. "What did you eat for breakfast? A bowl of hundred-pound weights with extra iron and vitamin C?!"

"Quit talking," I said, struggling to keep my balance. I looked up. Eyes on the prize, I thought as I slowly got to my feet.

I reached my arms up, but the human pyramid shook. I knelt back down fast so I wouldn't fall. "Hold still!"

"Hurry up!"

I got to my feet again. I reached up. The branch was still a few inches away. There was nothing for it. I would have to jump. I felt Roger shaking under me and T. J. under him. The pyramid wasn't going to last much longer.

I jumped just as Roger and T. J. toppled to the ground. My fingers touched bark and I held on tight.

"You did it, Fish!"

I dangled from the branch. I swung my legs over and slowly pulled myself up. PHEW!

"WOO-HOO!"

Roger and T. J. gave me the thumbs-up.

Champion Tatiana blinked her yellow cat eyes at me from the middle of the branch. Then she looked down on a manicured lawn and a gazebo. I could see a large, gray-shingled house in the distance with a tennis court on one side and a pool on the other. Below me was a pile of weeds.

There were some gardeners by the house, mowing the grass. They must have been responsible for the weeds, which also meant they would be coming back. We had to get out of here. I was definitely trespassing.

"Grab her and let's go," Roger called up to me.

I inched my way along the branch. Every inch I moved toward her, Champion Tatiana moved another inch away from me.

"It's okay, kitty," I said. "I'm here to help you."

She stopped at the sound of my voice and looked at me. I moved a little closer.

"Hold on," I said in the same soothing voice.

I moved a little closer. And a little closer. I was just about close enough to reach her. I stretched out my hand. My fingers were brushing her fur when a girl with long black hair burst out of the gazebo.

"You care more about your boat than about me!" she said into the cell phone at her ear. Then she angrily snapped it shut.

I don't know if she was startled by the girl's voice or if she just wanted to get out of my grasp, but Champion Tatiana jumped, landing on all fours at the girl's feet. The girl looked down at the cat and then up at the tree right at me. Her green eyes widened in surprise.

CRACK!

# YOU BET IT'S A BET!

"Fish! Fish!" came from the other side of the fence.

I lay there in the pile of weeds, staring up at the prettiest girl I had ever seen. She tossed her shiny brown hair and frowned down at me.

"Are you all right?"

I nodded. The weeds had cushioned my fall. I hopped to my feet, brushed off the dirt, and shook the leaves and grass from my hair.

The girl turned away, but not before I saw her wipe a tear off her cheek with the back of her hand. Why was she crying? I was pretty sure it wasn't because of Champion T and me. I had a hunch it had something to do with her phone call.

MEOW! Champion Tatiana stalked through the grass toward the house.

"Fish!" Roger and T. J. yelled again.

"Fish?" asked the girl, who looked less upset now. "She's *sooo* cute. Here, Fish! Here, Fish!"

Champion Tatiana turned and walked right up to her.

"How did you do that?" I asked.

"Oh, Fish, you are the sweetest kitty," cooed the girl, ignoring me.

She might be pretty, but she wasn't very friendly. Then again, I had crash-landed at her house without an invitation. I was just opening my mouth to tell her that Fish was my name when a voice called, "Clementine, are you ready to go?"

That voice sounded familiar. Before I could figure out who it was, the owner of the voice approached us. Dressed in tennis whites and wearing a brand-new pair of gold aviator sunglasses, he even wore a white sweatband with a Sandstone Club logo across his perfectly combed blond hair. "Fish Finelli, what in the heck are you doing here?!" said Bryce Billings. "You're trespassing big-time."

"You're Fish?!" said Clementine, looking at me in surprise. "I thought the cat was—"

"I was rescuing the cat," I said, staring at Clementine, who held Tatiana in her arms.

"She is so sweet. What's her name, if it's not Fish?"

"Champion Teeter-Tott—I mean, Champion Tatiana," I said. "She's a Cat Fancy Double Champion."

"Who cares?!" Bryce's gold glasses glinted in the sun. "Get lost! Like I said, you're trespassing."

Just because Bryce was a year older and lived here in the Lanes didn't mean he could talk to me like that. It wasn't as if I was trespassing on purpose, and it wasn't like this was his house. "You don't live here!" I said, my face turning red, the way it does when I start getting mad. "I don't have to listen to you."

"I live right next door," said Bryce. He spoke real slow, as if he were speaking to a little kid. "And my dad sold Clementine's dad this house." Bryce's dad owns the biggest real estate company around. That's where Roger's mom works. "On top of that, our families are old friends. Got it, loser?"

"I'm not a loser!" I snuck a glance at Clementine. She was busy cuddling Tatiana and didn't seem to be listening.

"YEAH! He's not a loser," called Roger from the other side of the fence.

WOOF! barked Shrimp.

"I see you brought your loser friends with you, like usual," said Bryce.

"We are not losers." I could feel my ears burning, like they do when I'm really mad.

"You will be when I beat you at the Captain Kidd Classic."

"That's a boat race, right?" Clementine looked over at us with sudden interest.

"Only the biggest boat race of the summer," said Bryce.

"Can anybody enter?" she asked.

"Anybody with a boat and a motor," said Bryce. "It's divided into classes by age group. And this loser has the crazy idea that he can beat me, even though I have more racing experience and a *way* better boat."

"Just you wait, Bryce," I said, my heart thudding in my chest. "You'll be eating our spray."

It was always my dream to enter a boat in the Classic, but like I said, Operation Fireball was also about beating Bryce. See, Bryce is the one who dared me to find Captain Kidd's treasure. That was our first bet, and I won, so Bryce had to give me his sunglasses. He was pretty mad, so he said some nasty stuff about my dad being a plumber. Then

## COMPASS

The magnetic compass was invented in China, and was first used for navigation in the 11th century. It works because the Earth is like a magnet (its inner core is made of iron and nickel), with two magnetic poles, one near the North Pole and one near the South Pole, that cause the compass's magnetized needle (made of iron or steel) to swing into a North/South position.

I got mad and told him in front of everybody that we would beat him at the Captain Kidd Classic. That's how our second bet started.

"Ha, ha! Is that still a bet, even though you know I am *so* going to bury you?"

"You bet it's a bet!" I said, louder than I meant to.

"Yeah!" said Roger and T. J. from the other side of the fence.

WOOF!

"Yeah, right!" snorted Bryce. "Your boat is a hunk of junk and your motor is so old it doesn't even run."

"The *Fireball* is not a hunk of junk!" Roger yelled.

The *Fireball* may be old, but it's still a good whaler. It's an eleven-footer just like Bryce's, except that his is brand-new. The Captain gave it to me two weeks ago for my tenth birthday, when I got my Boating Safety Certificate. That's the age you have to be to operate a motorboat on your own. You have to learn all this stuff about marine safety, like how you always pass another boat on the port (that's the left) side, and how the number one rule is to help any boater who gets in trouble. Then the Captain gave me another test with a crazy map to prove I could navigate with a compass. The Captain knows just about everything about boats. He used to be in the Navy. I passed his test, too. Now the boat is officially mine.

"How much horsepower is allowed in the race?" asked Clementine.

Whoa! So this girl was pretty and she knew about boats, too.

"Nine point nine!" we both said at the same time.

"Jinx!" said Roger from the other side of the fence.

Bryce rolled his eyes and we heard Roger snicker.

I tried not to think about Bryce's top-of-the-line whaler or his brand-new 9.9 horsepower Mercury Four Stroke motor. I also tried not to think about all of the bucket tests the Seagull motor had failed. Or the fact that even if it worked, the Seagull was only five horsepower, and we had to come up with some way to boost it to at least nine if we wanted to compete in the race and beat Bryce for real.

"Whatever, loser."

Bryce turned to Clementine and smiled real big, like he meant it. "My mom's going to drive us to the club to play tennis. I brought an extra racket for you."

Holy cannoli! The smile and the niceness were not the Bryce Billings I knew. That could only mean one thing. Bryce like-liked Clementine! The question was, did she like-like him back?

"Here," she said, handing Champion Tatiana to me. She looked like her mind was a million miles away.

"Thank you!" I said.

I wanted to say something else, but all I could think of was how I had fallen out of that tree and landed at her feet. My face started getting hot again.

"You can go through the gate this time," said Clementine, flipping her long, beautiful hair in my direction.

Clearly, she remembered my fall, too.

"Only birdbrains fall out of trees. Tweet tweet!" Bryce laughed and flapped his arms.

My face was now so burning hot, it was probably as red as a red snapper's dorsum (that's what a fish's back is called).

"Hey, tomato face!" Bryce rolled his eyes. "You are such a freak."

I tried not to get madder, because my face would only get redder. I wondered if Clementine thought I was a freak, too. I snuck a peek at her at the same moment she looked over at me. Instead of looking disgusted, she smiled this little smile only I could see.

"See ya," she said, and turned and headed toward her house. Bryce took a moment to make the L for loser sign at me with his thumb and forefinger. Then he ran to catch up to her.

I gritted my teeth. Now I really had to beat Bryce. After all, Clementine might come to the race. . . .

# HAPPY AS CLAMS

"Here we go again," said Roger, yawning as he batted a beach ball at T. J.

It was the next day and we were back in my garage. I had decided to take the Seagull apart and put it back together again. That's how it said to fix a washing machine motor in one of my dad's plumbing books. That book also said if you can fix a washing machine, you can fix a rocket launcher. It had to be a good way to fix a boat motor, too.

T. J. batted the ball back with one hand. WHOOSH! The ball skimmed the top of my head. Startled, I let go of the wrench I was using to remove the spark plugs.

CRASH! The throttle hit the floor. The rest of the motor fell, too. Oil spattered all over me and the garage floor.

"Oopsy daisy!" said Roger.

"Sorry!" said T. J.

"Guys! We promised my mom we wouldn't make a mess like yesterday."

T. J. and Roger came over to help pick up the pieces. We laid them on my dad's worktable and stared at them silently.

"I would like to say a few words in honor of the Seagull. The Seagull was a fine motor that never started," said Roger. Then he began to fake cry.

"Roger, quit talking like it's a funeral," I said, pulling the engine toward me. The propeller fell off.

"The Seagull just fell to pieces at the end." Roger went on fake crying.

I sighed and bent to pick up the propeller.

"Face it, dude," Roger laughed. "We need help."

"What about your dad or your uncle?" asked T. J.

"Busy. They have to install all these automatic flush toilets and sinks in the new art museum." I took a deep breath. "We can do this, guys. I know we can get this motor working."

*"Ohhh-kaaaay,"* said Roger. "But then what about the fact that it's only five horsepower and Bryce's is almost ten?

That's twice as much power, dude. And even though you got a perfect score on your Boating Safety Test, the numbers are the numbers. Ten trumps five every time."

"We can double our horsepower," I said. "I read all about it. We just have to blow out the cylinder somehow, get a bigger piston, and do something to the carburetor . . . I think. We might need a blowtorch to melt the metal, but we can figure that out when we get to it."

Roger raised his eyebrows. I stuck a screwdriver into one of the screws on the cylinder. I started to turn it. I lost my grip and the screwdriver flew out of my hand.

SPLAT! It landed in the bucket of night crawlers Uncle Norman was saving for a fishing trip.

"Fish, I hate to break it to you, but there are only two weeks till the Classic," said Roger. "If you want to win, we need professional help."

"We don't have money for professional help," I said. "Not after we spent all our money on the motor and new steering wheel for the *Fireball*. Right, T. J.?"

T. J., who was our unofficial treasurer and in charge of the money, nodded.

"How much do we have exactly?"

"Nine dollars and sixty-three cents," said T. J. "Just about enough for a large pie with extra cheese."

"T. J., we don't need food," I said.

"No, what we need is a mechanic who will work for nine dollars and sixty-three cents," said Roger. "And since that's not happening, I think Teej is right. We might as well get a pizza with pepperoni."

"And peppers," said T. J.

"And pineapple," said Roger.

"No way," said T. J. "Pineapple is nasty on pizza. It's . . . it's . . . un-American."

"Since pizza is Italian, I don't think that matters," said Roger. "And it's not nasty, it's de-lish."

"Guys," I said. "Will you stay on toppings—I mean, topic?"

T. J. and Roger laughed.

"It's not funny."

"Yes it is, Fish. And we are on topic. The topic is toppings."

"I'm serious," I said.

"I know you're serious," said Roger. "You are in serious need of lightening up."

"I don't need to lighten up. I need help with this motor."

"I've got it!" said T. J., a big smile on his face. "Clams!"

"Now, clams on pizza are what I call nasty," said Roger.

"Enough with the toppings, guys!"

"T. J.'s right, Finelli," said Roger. "Clams are just what we need. Clams as in moolah, dough, money."

"I meant the Clam Brothers," said T. J.

"Mi and Si?" I said. Micah and Silas King were twins a year older than us. They ran a clam stand every summer on Two Mile Harbor. Their dad was a fisherman.

"We don't need them," said T. J. "We need Eli, their second-oldest brother. He got a job at the marina. My aunt wants my cousin Tater to work there."

"Your cousin Couch Po-Tater?" said Roger. "Or, should I say *Tater Tot*? I thought watching TV was his only hobby."

"Not anymore. My aunt gave away his TV and his computer."

"Why would Eli help us?" I asked. "I mean, it's not like we have the money to pay him."

"I bet Eli would love to work on a motor. You know, like how firefighters burn down old houses just to practice." T. J. pulled a squished cinnamon bun out of his pocket and began to chew.

I looked at the busted-up motor. Maybe T. J. was right. The truth was, a little help would be helpful.

"All right," I said. "Let's go see Mi and Si. We can find out if they think Eli would even consider helping us." It wasn't as if we could just go to the marina and ask Eli, since he was in high school and we didn't exactly *know him* know him.

"This could be just the thing to get Operation Fireball off the ground," said Roger. "And we've got nothing to lose. Right, Fish?"

+ + +

I found out pretty quick just what I had to lose. . . .

"I am *not* giving you my Superman Special Shooter." I frowned at Mi, who was busy counting a wad of dollar bills.

"Twenty-one, twenty-two. It's not a gift," said Mi, thumbing through the money. "Thirty, thirty-one. It's a trade." He kept counting and didn't even look up.

We were at the Clam Brothers' clam stand. Just a few turns past the marina, you can't miss it. A surfboard propped up against a telephone pole says CLAMS in big red letters. The Clam Brothers have been running the stand for years, since the oldest brother, Jared, who's so old he's in college, was a little kid. Mi and Si took over after Eli got the marina job.

Just then we heard the hum of a car coming around the curve.

"Si, hold up the sign!" said Mi.

Si jumped on top of a cooler and held up a cardboard sign: CLAMS . . . $5 PER DOZEN.

One of those big old Cadillacs from the 1960s with white-wall tires and pointy fins on the sides pulled up. A woman with a tall hairdo and lots of lipstick the same bright pink color as the car stuck her head out. "Yoo-hoo, boys! I'd like a dozen clams."

Si hopped off the cooler and popped the lid.

"Get her a dozen," said Mi, pointing at us.

"We don't work for you," I said.

"You want our help? Then you've got to help us."

Mi handed me a plastic bag and T. J., Roger, and I counted out twelve clams. They sure were slimy. We gave the bag to the lady. Mi came and took her five dollars.

"So, are you going to hand over the Superman Special Shooter or not?" asked Mi.

"C'mon, Fish," said T. J. "It'll be worth it. Just think of the Seagull."

"I don't like it, but I think it's the only way," Roger whispered in my ear. "Hey, it's just a marble."

The Superman Special Shooter wasn't just a marble. It was an awesome collector marble from the 1950s. It was blue, yellow, and red—the colors of Superman. I had won it off Two O at the end of the school year. He supposedly got it from his grandpa, who won it off some kid when he was a kid. Two O's real name is Owen Osborn, by the way, but everybody calls him Two O, even the principal.

"Here." I pulled the marble out of my pocket. "You going to take us to Eli now?"

Mi held up the marble between his thumb and index finger, examining it in the sunlight. "Yep, a deal's a deal. And the Clam Brothers always honor a deal."

Roger hopped on his bike. "Last one there's a rotten banana!"

T. J. and I helped Mi and Si load the clams onto their red wagon. By the time we got going, Roger was long gone.

The Clam Brothers rode behind T. J. and me on an old two-seater bike, pulling the wagon.

When we reached the marina, Roger was waiting for us in front of the office. He had a goofy smile on his face as he pointed to a poster advertising the Captain Kidd Classic— the oldest motorboat race in Whooping Hollow—circa 1933. There was a drawing on it of Captain Kidd looking like a real pirate, with a kerchief and a black hat on his head and a big gold earring in his ear, standing next to a treasure chest stuffed with jewels.

Everybody thinks Captain Kidd was a pirate, but he was really a privateer hired to catch pirates. He didn't look anything like that, either. I saw a picture of him at the library. He had long, lumpy white hair, kind of like George Washington, which I bet was really a wig.

"And the winner is . . . da-da-da-da . . . the *Fireball!*" Roger bowed.

I sure wished we would win. First prize for each age group was $100 and a silver cup. Uncle Norman and my dad won when they were my age. My dad still has the cup.

"I would like to thank my family and everyone here at the marina for all of their support," Roger went on in a loud voice.

The docks were crowded. A bunch of people turned around to look.

"Most of all I would like to thank my team—I couldn't have done it without them," Roger said. "Come on up here, boys. Take a bow. Don't be shy."

"Roger!" I said. "Will you quit it?!"

Roger put his arm around me. "See this boy, ladies and gentlemen." More people turned. "This boy had a dream that one day he would have a boat and he stopped at nothing to make that dream a reality so he could enter the Captain—OOMPH!"

I elbowed him hard as people laughed.

"See you at the Classic!" said Roger. "May the best racers win!"

Everyone laughed again and went back to what they were doing except for a tall, tanned man with silver-blond hair. He was dressed in a fancy suit and carrying a shiny leather briefcase. He was not smiling as he headed toward the marina office. We jumped out of the way as he flung open the door and strode inside.

"I came here as soon as I got to town," he said. "Where is the princess?"

"*Princess*?" said Roger. "I didn't know we had royalty in town."

We all shrugged.

"I should never have trusted the princess with some local kid," said the man in an angry voice.

"Mr. de Quincy," said Mr. Blue, the marina manager. "I'm sure Eli would only treat the princess with the utmost care and consideration. We can go check on her right now if you'd like."

"Uh-oh," said Si, with a look at Mi.

"We better go find Li," said Mi.

"He never said anything about a princess," said Si.

The Clam Brothers ran to a shed at the far end of the marina. We hurried after them. Inside we found someone dressed in a white jumpsuit, white gloves, goggles, and a mask. The person was sanding a small patch of cherry-red paint along the hull. The boat had a shiny wooden transom to match the shiny wooden cockpit; she was an awesome boat!

BUZZ! BUZZ!

"Li!" Mi and Si said over the pulsing of the sander. "Li!"

Eli turned it off and pulled off his goggles.

"What did you do with the princess?" Mi asked in a panicked voice.

"Your boss is coming to look for her right now," said Si. "You're going to get it."

Eli laughed and patted the hull of the boat he was sanding. "Meet the princess, boys."

"The princess is a boat?!" said T. J. "Holy cow!"

"She's amazing," I said.

Eli nodded. "Princess powerboats are some of the finest ever made."

Just then we heard a voice. "Ah, here is the princess, Mr. de Quincy. I think you'll find her in peak condition."

"Scram, guys," said Eli. "Meet me on the back dock in ten."

We sneaked around the side of the boat. As we headed out the opposite end of the shed, I took one last look at the princess. She was the most beautiful boat I had ever seen. That's when I noticed the name in gold cursive letters painted on the port side: *Clementine.*

WHOA! Clementine, as in Clementine the girl whose backyard I had fallen into?!

It had to be her. I mean, how many Clementines could there be in one little town? I remembered what she had said about someone caring more about a boat than about her. I bet Mr. de Quincy was her dad.

We skipped stones while we waited. I thought I was good, but Mi could do six in a row every time.

Finally, Eli jogged toward us. "So, what do you guys want?"

"These guys need some help with a motor," said Mi, nodding at us.

"What kind of motor?"

"A Seagull," I said. "It's a Silver Century Plus, from the seventies."

Eli whistled. "Wow! I've never seen one of those. Their propellers are legendary. Used to power light assault craft during the Second World War. Motor's real quiet."

I nodded, although I had never actually heard the motor.

"Does it run?"

T. J., Roger, and I shook our heads.

"If Li agrees to help, it's going to cost you," said Mi.

Eli knocked Mi playfully on the arm. "This kid is all about business."

"So, first things first," said Mi. "We need to agree on a price."

"The thing is, we don't really have any money," I said.

"Are you kidding me?!" said Mi, throwing up his hands. "Why didn't you tell me that before?"

"That's not exactly true," said Roger. "We have nine dollars and sixty-three cents."

Mi laughed. "That's less than we get for two dozen clams!"

Eli looked from Mi to me and then out at the harbor, where a fishing boat was pulling up to the pier. On the deck a bunch of fish were flopping around in nets. "I have an idea," said Eli. "How about you guys go clamming for me? If you can dig up my share of clams, I can use that time to work on your motor. It will be good experience for me."

"Really?"

Eli nodded.

"So, you guys find a hundred clams, and then Li will look at your motor," said Mi. He pulled a pad and a pen out of his pocket and started making notes.

"That's way too many clams, Mi," said Eli.

"What about ninety?" said Si.

"No, I think fifty would be good," said Eli. "Deal?"

I nodded. "The thing is, we also need to up the horsepower from five to nine point nine."

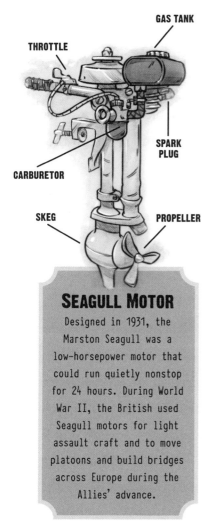

THROTTLE

GAS TANK

SPARK PLUG

CARBURETOR

SKEG

PROPELLER

## SEAGULL MOTOR

Designed in 1931, the Marston Seagull was a low-horsepower motor that could run quietly nonstop for 24 hours. During World War II, the British used Seagull motors for light assault craft and to move platoons and build bridges across Europe during the Allies' advance.

"For the Classic, huh?"

I nodded again.

"If I bore out the cylinder, I can put in a bigger piston, and the extra space will allow more air and more gas into the combustion chamber."

"Huh?" said Roger, T. J., Mi, and Si.

"More air and more gas equals more power." I grinned at Eli.

"Sounds expensive," said Mi, making another note on his pad. "It'll cost you more."

"No, it won't," said Eli. "Actually, I would love to experiment with a Seagull motor, since I've never worked on one before. Maybe I'll change out the carburetor, too."

"So, that's fifty clams by closing tomorrow night," said Mi, making a note on his pad. "Then Li will look at your motor."

"You guys know how to clam?" asked Eli, smiling at us.

"It takes some real skill," said Mi. "And experience, of course. You gotta know how to sign."

Roger rubbed his chin with his fingers, as if he were deep in thought. "Not a problem. I think this is a sign that we're all going to be happy as clams!"

# CLAM-DUNK!

"T. J., Roger. It's three o'clock, and low tide is at three twenty-five, so we need to get moving if we're going to find a good spot before then."

"I'm telling you, clamming is a no-brainer," Roger said, popping a wheelie down Sandy Lane.

"Actually, it is true that bivalve mollusks like clams have no brains," I said, balancing the bucket across my handlebars.

"See, the little dummies will be easy to catch," said Roger. "They don't have the brain power to come up with a getaway plan."

It was the next day, and we were heading to Sandstone Cove to go clamming. We had stopped by the Captain's to pick up some PFDs (Personal Flotation Devices). The

Captain said Sandstone Cove was an excellent spot for clamming because nobody went there. You can't beach a boat because the water's too shallow and there's no access from the road. He also said if we hit a SNAFU (Situation Normal All Fouled Up, in Navy speak), we should abort the mission. Sometimes the Captain thinks he's still in the Navy.

When we reached the end of Sandy Lane, the Sandstone Club loomed on the hill ahead of us. It was three stories with weathered gray shingles, a bunch of chimneys, and tall white columns. A long white-pebbled driveway curved up to it. Not a single white pebble was in the perfectly mowed, super green grass of the golf course that stretched out all around it. Mr. O, Two O's dad, who is the golf course manager, made sure of that. As if just thinking about him made him appear, he putt-putted by in his Sandstone Club golf cart. We could tell it was him because it says MANAGER on the side of the cart.

"We'd better get going," said Roger.

T. J. and I nodded. Mr. O doesn't like kids anywhere near his championship greens. Two O got mad at his dad one time and pogo-sticked right across the fairway. He was grounded for six whole months.

We rode past the far edge of the course. I caught a glimpse of the tennis courts. I wondered if Clementine was there somewhere playing tennis. And if Bryce was with her.

We kept riding south-southwest, according to the Captain's directions. It only took a few minutes to spot the Lily Pond.

"Okay, we need to go east now," I said, turning right.

There were no houses, no road, not even a trail. I pulled up to the edge of the weeds. Just past them I could see some scrubby trees and dune grass. T. J. and Roger pulled up beside me.

"We're going to have to leave our bikes here." I wheeled mine into the weeds. I grabbed the bucket off the handle-bars and the shovel I had stuck in the rack.

T. J. opened up one of the bags hanging off the back of his bike. He pulled out a plastic, kiddy-sized rake, shovel, and hoe.

"We're clamming, dude," I said. "Not gardening."

T. J. shrugged. "It was all I could find in the bathtub. I figured a rake's a rake, right?"

The bathtub is this gigantic old Jacuzzi tub in the Mahoneys' garage, where T. J.'s mom makes his dad keep all of the stuff he picks up on carting jobs that he thinks is too useful to throw away. T. J.'s dad owns a waste-removal company called Mahoney's Carting. All the trucks have a picture of a garbage can with gold and jewels coming out, with the slogan WE TREASURE YOUR TRASH written underneath.

"Rog, you ready?" I asked.

Roger peeked inside his backpack, smiled mysteriously, and zipped it up.

"What you got, dude?" I asked.

He just shook his head and smiled again.

The three of us pushed through the weeds, past the scrub pine trees to a small strip of beach around a pond. To the side was a patch of cattails, just like the Captain had instructed. Cattails always grow by water. The Native Americans used to eat the bulbs and the stems.

The deserted beach and Sandy Bay stretched out beyond.

"Sweet!" said Roger. "Our own private beach."

"Time to clam, guys," I said, leading the way to the cattails.

Roger unzipped his backpack with a flourish. He whipped out a long, gray plastic tube that looked like a section of plumber's pipe.

"HI-YA!" He rammed the tube into the sand.

"What are you doing with that pipe?" I asked.

"That's not a pipe," said Roger. "It's a gun."

"A gun?!"

"Yep," said Roger. "I'm clamming with it."

"You can't clam with a gun!"

"It's a clam gun. I found it in the basement. My dad brought it back from Alaska when he went there to do a story about Alaskan sports."

"Clamming is a sport in Alaska?" I said.

"Guess so." Roger smiled, but his eyes looked sad. Roger's dad is a sportswriter and he travels all over the world. He gives Roger the sickest stuff, like a Derek Jeter rookie card worth over $500 and a real New York Knicks basketball jersey and the newest-model skateboards. The thing is, since his parents' divorce Roger hardly ever sees him. Even though Roger never says so, I know he misses his dad a lot.

Roger pulled up the clam gun and took his finger off an airhole on the side. A bunch of sand shot out of the tube.

"Get any clams?" said T. J.

"Not yet. POW! POW! POW! Just you wait."

I had done a little reading on clamming and I didn't remember anything about guns. I had learned a bunch of stuff about how to sign for clams. You have to look for little airholes in the sand. Clams make the holes when they filter water for food. I also learned that clams are usually an inch or so down, which is why sometimes it's easiest to just feel for them with your feet. If the water isn't too deep, you can pick them up with your toes.

"Man your battle stations." Roger ran into the water, waving the clam gun around. "Load your CLAMmunition!"

T. J. followed, pulling a handful of what looked like Jujubes out of his pocket and tossing them at Roger. "Think clams like candy?"

"They don't have mouths to eat with," I said. "Or noses to smell with. They sift water through tubes to find microscopic organisms called plankton. That's their source of nutrition."

Just then something wet and slimy hit me on the arm.

"Enough with the life science lesson, dude," said Roger. "It's CLAMnoying."

He and T. J. laughed. I tossed the seaweed back. Roger ducked and the seaweed hit T. J. on the head. He grabbed for it and fell backward into the shallows.

I looked down at the sand. I couldn't believe my eyes. There were little holes. I bent down and started to dig. My shovel hit something hard. I pulled it out.

"Hey, guys. I found a clam! We only need forty-nine more."

The clam smelled pretty stinky because the shell was open, but I slipped it in my pocket anyway. I wondered for a second if the shell being open meant it was dead, but I figured it didn't matter. A clam was a clam.

"Catch, Roger!" called T. J., lobbing a seaweed-covered lump at him.

"Ouch."

"That rock sure is prickly. Good catch," said T. J.

"This isn't a rock," said Roger, rubbing off the sand. "It's a clam."

"Let me see." I waded over to Roger.

The shell was purple and white and there were barnacles all over it.

"That's not a clam," I said. "It's an oyster!"

"Too bad, because there are lots of them over here," said T. J.

"YES!!! Oysters are better than clams. They're worth twice as much. Bet that will make the Clam Brothers happy."

"Clams are out, oysters are in," said Roger.

We spent the next hour digging up oysters, wading farther and farther into the water until it was almost up to our waists. They were easy to find with our toes. Unlike clams, oysters don't have feet to move around, so there were lots of them together.

I felt a lump and gripped it with my toes. Then I started pulling it up. I was just reaching down to grab it when my toes lost their grip. SPLASH! It fell back into the water.

"Rats!" I said.

"Another one bites the dust," said Roger as he pulled another oyster out from between his toes. I swear his toes are like lobster's pincer claws. He never dropped a single one. Even though T. J. and I had dropped some, the three of us had still managed to find so many that we had to leave the bucket in the shallows because it was so heavy.

PLINK! PLINK! PLINK!

**OYSTER**

This invertebrate (no spine) bivalve mollusk (enclosed in two shells) is not related to the pearl oyster. It is three to fourteen inches long, gray, slimy, and high in calcium, protein, and iron. It extracts algae and food particles from water it draws over its gills, filtering up to 1.3 gallons of water per hour.

"Check out this jump shot," said Roger, splashing water all over us as he jumped up and threw another oyster in the bucket.

PLINK!

"Mahoney shoots a three-pointer from the line!" T. J. aimed high and threw.

PLINK! went the oyster into the bucket.

"Who knew Clam Ball could be so much fun?" asked Roger.

Just as the bucket was almost full, we heard a growing hum. We turned to see three boats racing across the bay. The hum raised in pitch, getting louder as the one with the red stripe that was way in the lead skimmed the surface. It looked like a Whaler Super Sport, and I bet it had twenty or even thirty horsepower to go so fast. Ten horsepower was nothing compared to that, but kids our age pretty much weren't allowed to drive boats with so much speed till we were older, unless there was an adult on board.

My mouth dropped open as I watched the red boat's hull rise into the air. The propeller was practically the only part of the boat that was still in the water.

"Snap!" said Roger. "That boat is flying!"

I nodded. "It's called planing. We need to try to do that, too, if we want to win the Classic."

"How do you do it?" asked T. J.

"It happens when the speed of the boat pushing the hull out of the water is equal to the force exerted by the water on the bottom of the hull," I said.

"In English, genius," said Roger.

"Just like how a plane flies," I said. "On account of the force of the air pressure pushing against the wings. I'm pretty sure that's how come it's called planing."

"Who cares what it's called?" said Roger. "It's awesome!"

We were so busy watching the red boat zooming over the waves that we didn't notice the smaller white boat with the green stripe zipping toward us. There was a third boat with a blue stripe just behind it.

"Get off our beach!"

I didn't have to see the name painted on the side to know it was the *Viper*. Or the gold sunglasses on the face of the boy at the wheel to know it was Bryce. His best friend, Trippy, snickered beside him. Clementine was behind them. She wore a red bathing suit and the same serious expression she had when she looked at me lying on the pile of weeds in her yard.

"This isn't your beach!" I shouted.

"Yeah!" said Roger and T. J.

"Beat it, clam diggers!" Bryce pulled out the throttle and swerved closer.

Waves rocketed toward us. Salty water shot up and filled my nose, eyes, and mouth. Behind us the oyster bucket tipped over. Roger splashed over to pick it up. Trippy and the other boys in the blue boat laughed. I noticed they were all wearing Sandstone Club sweatbands.

Bryce swerved again, making the water splash all over us. Clementine held on unhappily to the rail.

"You don't own this beach!" I said.

"It's club property," said Bryce. "And since you don't belong to the club, you don't belong here."

"It is not," I said. "It belongs to the town, like all the beaches do. We have every right to be here."

"Well, maybe we just don't want you around, birdbrain," said Bryce. "I think it's time for you to go find your tree! Tweet! Tweet!"

"Tweet! Tweet!" echoed the other boys.

"These clam diggers think they're going to beat me at the Classic," said Bryce. "You should see their boat. It's an old wreck that will probably break down in the middle of the race."

The boy at the wheel of the blue-striped boat laughed. "There should be a rule that only cool, new boats like ours can enter."

"Good idea, True," said Trippy, giving the boy a thumbs-up. True, unlike Bryce and Trippy, must have been a summer boy, because I had never seen him before.

"Yeah, that would keep losers and their cheap boats out of the way," said Bryce.

"You know, winning isn't just about having the most expensive boat," said Clementine. "It's also about having the skill to maneuver it."

Was Clementine sticking up for me?

"Whatever," said Bryce. "The fact is, birdbrain, you and your dork friends don't stand a chance against us in the race. You should quit now before we slay you. "

I hate being told I can't do something. It makes me madder than anything. I was so mad right then that all I could think about was how much I wanted to wipe that smug smile off Bryce's face. I reached into my pocket for something to throw and pulled out the first thing I touched.

"Just you wait, Bryce. You'll see. Now leave us alone!" I started yanking on the split in the clamshell.

"Yeah!" said Roger and T. J., coming to stand beside me.

"You can't tell me what to do, Clam Digger!"

"Oh, yeah?"

I gave the clamshell one more hard yank. CRACK! It split open enough for me to pull out the slimy clam inside. Roger and T. J. gagged beside me. It stank something awful.

"Yeah, loooooser!"

I pulled back my arm, aimed, and let go.

SPLAT!

The clam hit Bryce on the forehead right between the eyes. Smelly clam slime oozed down his face and into his mouth.

"PTOOEY!" Bryce made a face and spit it out.

"EW, dude!" said True.

"You stink!" said Trippy.

Clementine had a hand over her mouth, as if she were trying to cover up a smile and cover her nose at the same time.

"Clam-dunk, Finelli!" said Roger.

Bryce wiped the clam gunk off his face and glared at me, sputtering mad. "You're going to be sorry, Clam Digger!"

Then he wound up to hurl the clam.

"Duck!" shouted Roger.

None of us wasted another second. T. J. took off first. Roger and I grabbed the bucket of oysters and ran after him. We could hear splashing sounds behind us. It was either stuff Bryce and his friends were throwing our way, or maybe they were coming after us themselves. We had to get out of there, and fast.

Roger and I got to our bikes a second after T. J. "How are we going to carry the bucket on a bike?" Roger panted, trying to catch his breath. "It's really heavy."

"Unload it," I gasped, reaching into the bucket. "T. J., here, put a bunch of oysters in your pockets and in your bike bags. Roger, put them in your backpack. I'll carry the rest in the bucket."

"Hurry!" said Roger. "They could be here any second."

We had just gotten onto our bikes and I was trying to balance the bucket between my handlebars when there was a crashing sound behind us. We looked up in time to see Bryce and Trippy bursting through the weeds.

"Go!" I pushed off and pedaled like crazy.

Roger and T. J. took off, too. We didn't slow down till the club and Sandy Lane were long past and we had reached the harbor. By then we were sweaty, sandy, and exhausted. It was just past five o'clock. Si was packing up the wagon and Mi was counting the money.

"Dudes, what happened to you?" said Mi, looking us up and down. "Run-in with some tough clams?"

"As a matter of fact, Bryce and Trippy," said Roger, jumping off his bike.

"Ouch!" said Mi.

"I can't wait till we beat them in the Classic," I said, dropping my bike and grabbing the bucket. "Check out what we found."

"It's your lucky day, guys," said Roger, opening up his backpack.

Mi and Si peered inside. I handed them the bucket and T. J. pulled more oysters out of his bags and pockets. Their eyes almost popped out of their heads.

"Oysters?! Dudes, you rock! We haven't had any oysters in weeks."

Si high-fived each of us.

"I didn't know you were planning to go up against Bryce Billings," said Mi, a glint of admiration in his eyes. "He's got that sick new whaler, and . . ." His voice trailed off. "Dude, the Clam Brothers are *so* going to help you on your mission."

Si nodded solemnly at his brother's words.

"You can bring the motor to the marina now. Eli is working late."

T. J., Roger, and I got back on our bikes.

"I hope you beat Bryce Billings," said Mi. "I don't think you have a snowball's chance in a campfire, but . . ." He paused and held up a slimy clam. "I solemnly swear on the clam that whatever the Clam Brothers can do to help, we'll do." He handed the clam to Si.

"Ditto. I solemnly swear on the clam. . . ."

# IT'S A BIRD. IT'S A PLANE.
# IT'S THE *FIREBALL!*

Three days later, Roger, T. J., and I were on our way to pick up the Seagull.

"I can't wait to see how Eli bored out the cylinder and put in the bigger piston." I smiled as I pulled the wagon along the dock. Most boats were already tied up for the night since it was after seven, so it was pretty quiet.

"Hey, let's go check the sign-up sheet for the race," I said, dropping the wagon handle and running up the steps to the marina office. There were eight racers in each race class, and the classes were divided by age group: eleven and under, which was our class; twelve- to fourteen-year-olds; and fifteen- to eighteen-year-olds. I knew Bryce and Two O were racing for sure, as well as this fifth-grader named Max, who was a sailor but who wanted to try a motorboat race.

Bryce's friend, True, who we met when we were clamming, was in the race, too, last I checked, along with three other summer kids I didn't know, but there was still no eighth racer.

"Oooh, looks like we've got a number eight," said Roger, elbowing me out of the way.

"Hey," I said. "Let me see. Who is it?"

Roger moved his shoulder to block my view.

"Z something," said T. J., peering over Roger's other shoulder.

"What kind of name is that?"

"Zat is ze question," said Roger.

T. J. shrugged. "Z something I can't pronounce is the name of the boat. There's nothing listed under racer's name."

"Guys!" called Mi, running up to us. "C'mon!"

I forgot all about the eighth racer, as we hurried after him to the same shed where Eli had been working on the princess. This time he wasn't wearing goggles, though.

He finished tightening one of the spark plugs below the Seagull's fuel tank. Then he wiped the grease off his hands with a rag. There were tools and engine parts all over the place.

"It's all set," he said, giving the Seagull a final rub with his rag. "Runs nice and quiet, too. You had fixed it, and

it would have run, but a little bit of rust was clogging up the fuel tank. The original four-bladed propeller is in good condition. It's excellent in any kind of rough water. I tweaked the blade of the pitch, too, so that should up the horsepower one or two points."

"Funny how it still looks the same," said Roger, scratching his head.

"On the outside, but not on the inside," I said. "Did you change the carburetor?"

"No. Shaving the cylinder to allow a greater volume of air and fuel, plus the bigger piston, should boost your power. Oh, and I got you some high-octane fuel to put in your tank on race day, which should give you a little bit more speed." He pointed to a red canister by his feet.

"Racing fuel! Wow! Thanks, Eli." I stared in awe from the fuel to the motor. "I don't know how I can ever repay you. . . ."

Eli shrugged. "Hey, seventy-two oysters at ten dollars a dozen is—"

"Sixty bucks," said Mi. "Not too shabby, dudes. Not too shabby at all. You can clam for the Clam Brothers anytime—you can be our new Oyster Division."

Si nodded.

"Only if you cut us in for fifty percent," said Roger.

"Fifty percent? Are you kidding me, Huckleton?" said Mi.

The two of them started to argue about what was fair.

Eli turned to me. "I want to show you how I fixed the clamps so you can attach the Seagull tightly to your boat. It's a whaler, right?"

I nodded. "An eleven-footer from the seventies. We fixed it up with some help from the Captain, who gave it to me."

"The Captain who lives out by Whale Rock?"

I nodded. Eli whistled. "You're lucky, dude. The Captain knows everything about boats. He sailed a destroyer during the Second World War."

"And a minesweeper and a torpedo boat," I said.

"So, how was the whaler? Hull cracked?" asked Eli.

"Yep. The Captain helped us seal the cracks, sand the decks a bunch of times, and put on like five coats of epoxy, primer, and paint. And we got a new wheel."

"Excellent." Eli pointed to the clamps on the motor. "Once you secure the clamps to the transom, I think it's a good idea to tie the motor to the boat with a lanyard, too.

And make sure the Seagull's tilted so that the propeller is at the right depth. The exhaust outlet should be no more than an inch or two below the surface of the water."

He tilted the motor to show me what he meant, and then helped me load it in the wagon. The Seagull is awkward to carry, but it's not all that heavy. It weighs about thirty-eight pounds, just a few more pounds than Feenie.

Eli stood there for a minute, thinking. "You know, getting up on plane may be hard with the weight of three of you in the boat, even with the boost in horsepower."

I nodded. From a purely mathematical point of view, it made the most sense for only one of us to race because the least amount of weight would most easily allow the bow to tip up and the hull to rise. I imagined myself alone at the wheel, cruising around the buoys at the Classic, the crowd roaring.

Then I looked over at Rog and Teej, laughing with Mi and Si. I realized that even though I wanted to beat Bryce more than anything, I wouldn't be racing at all if it weren't for them. It was the three of us or none of us. We'd figure out a way to get the *Fireball* to plane. Eli hadn't said it was impossible.

"Thanks for everything, Eli."

He smiled without looking up, already hard at work on another motor. I watched him remove a brand-new three-bladed propeller.

"What's wrong with the prop?" I couldn't help asking.

Eli shrugged. "People think a bigger prop is better because it makes a boat go faster, but if it makes the engine rev too fast, it will actually blow out the motor."

"Wow! I never knew that."

"Hey, Finelli, time to make like a drum and beat it," said Roger.

"You mean make like a tree and leave," said Mi.

"What about make like a bee and buzz?" asked T. J.

Si shook his head and laughed at the three of them.

"How about make like an atom and split?" I said, pulling the wagon over to where they were waiting for me.

"Very funny, Einstein."

"You know, Einstein is the scientist who split the atom by coming up with the formula $E = mc^2$."

"No!" said Roger, grabbing me and pulling me toward him. "He's turning into a mad scientist again. Only noogies will save him."

He, T. J., Mi, and Si all began rubbing their knuckles over my head.

"Guys, stop!" I said. Noogies tickle when they're not done too hard, or maybe I just have a very ticklish head.

"Good luck in the race, Fish!" said Eli.

We headed back along the dock as the sun sank behind the trees. Cicadas were chirping, and the sky was purple-blue like an oyster shell.

"See you tomorrow," said Mi, as T. J., Roger, and I turned toward Main Street.

"We'll bring a stopwatch to time you," added Si.

"Oh-nine-hundred hours," said Mi. "Be there or be square."

"Huh?" said T. J.

"Oh-nine-hundred hours means nine o'clock in the morning," I said. "It's military time."

"Don't be late!" Roger said.

"Punctuality is the Clam Brothers' middle name," Mi said before he and Si disappeared around the bend.

+ + +

Mi wasn't kidding. He and Si were right on time the next morning when they met us at the Captain's dock. It's always been one of my favorite places because you can see all the boats going by.

I took a moment to look proudly at the *Fireball*. It had taken the three of us and the Captain a while, but the seats had been sanded and stained to shiny brown wood. The interior was shiny blue. We had even painted the name FIREBALL on the starboard side with metallic red and yellow paint. The letters dripped some, so you kind of had to squint to read the words, but it still looked cool.

"Ready." I yanked on the reef knot I put in the lanyard to secure the motor the way Eli had instructed. Earlier that morning, the Captain had helped me hook up the fuel and steering cables to the gearbox beside the new wheel. I double-checked the clamps one more time to make sure they were tight.

"Ready," said Roger, holding up three PFDs and the Bug Patrol Emergency Backpack/Detective Kit. It's this bright orange backpack where we keep our bug-catching supplies and our detective stuff, like a flashlight, empty plastic containers for evidence or insects, dusting powder, a notebook, and rubber gloves. Now it also held a first-aid kit.

"Ready," said T. J., holding up a big brown paper bag. Veggie chips poked out of the top.

"T. J., no food," I said. "We have to have as little weight as possible to get up on plane."

"Even healthy stuff like veggie chips?" He sighed, but he put down the bag.

"Let's do this!" said Si, holding a stopwatch.

Mi picked up the bag of chips and tore them open. "Hmm. These actually taste pretty good, Mahoney. . . . Now, to Whale Rock and back."

I hopped in first to start the motor. I pulled on the rope to turn the flywheel clockwise, shut the throttle down to avoid racing, and opened the choke. The Seagull roared to life.

I grinned as Roger and T. J. hopped into the *Fireball* and I took my place at the wheel. Roger sat just ahead of me and T. J. was just behind. I pulled out the throttle.

"Ready," said Mi.

"Set," said Si.

## WIDOW'S WALK

A decorative rooftop platform popular during the 19th century, some say it got its name from when men went to sea. Their wives would watch for their return from the roofs of their houses, hoping to spot the sails of the ships. Because whaling was dangerous, men sometimes died at sea, leaving widows at home to mourn.

"Go!"

There was a popping sound. We looked up. A red and green flare shot over our heads. The Captain waved from the widow's walk.

"Press on!" he shouted through his bullhorn. That's Navy speak for get going and good luck.

The boat shot forward and I pulled out the throttle to full. We went faster. I steered straight for Whale Rock, but we weren't going fast enough. I could feel the drag behind us pulling us down.

"Lean forward!" I shouted, hoping that would get us up on plane by shifting the weight.

Roger leaned toward the bow. T. J. leaned toward me. I pulled the throttle out again. But it was out as far as it could go. Whale Rock was just ahead of us, but we still weren't on plane. It was probably because there was too much weight aft (that means to the back) of the boat. We would have to move some weight farther forward.

"To the bow!" I said, as we headed back.

Roger moved to the front of the boat and sat right on the bow.

"Hey, I'm getting all wet!" he called, as water splashed up around him.

It was no use anyway. We still couldn't get up on plane. I slowed down the engine as we got closer to the dock.

"Five minutes and thirty-six seconds," said Si.

"Not fast enough if you want to beat Bryce," said Mi.

"I know. We have to get up on plane."

I turned the boat around to try again. We had to improve our time. The first rule of planing was weight distribution, so clearly our weight was not distributed correctly.

"T. J., bow!" I said.

"Huh?" said T. J., taking a bite of Peppermint Pattie.

"Bow, *now!*"

T. J. stood up and bowed.

Si and Mi clapped.

"T. J., c'mon!" I said, trying not to get mad.

"What? You said 'Bow,' so I bowed."

"I meant to go sit in the bow."

T. J. climbed over the seat and squashed himself behind Roger, who was still sitting on the bow.

"Roger, you sit behind me," I said.

Once Roger was in position, the *Fireball* felt more balanced. I knew a boat had to sit level to plane, but I wondered how the bow was going to be able to lift with T. J.'s weight right on top of it. It needed to rise from two to seven degrees to develop the lift it needed to plane.

"Teej, move off the bow a little toward the middle."

T. J. positioned himself between the bow and the wheel. "It's kind of like musical chairs, without the chairs," he said.

"Or the music," said Roger.

"To get up on plane, we need the hull to climb over and pass its own bow wave," I said. "The hull needs to lift off the water, reducing drag and increasing speed."

"Okay, guys. Ready?" said Mi, his expression as serious now as when he counts money.

"Set . . ." said Si.

"Go!"

I pulled out the throttle and the *Fireball* shot forward. The hull started to lift up.

"Move back more, Teej!" I called.

T. J. scooted toward me, pressing his back against the gearbox. I pulled the throttle all the way out. The hull rose up that next few degrees, and we were gliding over the waves. We did it. We were on plane! It felt like we were flying. Maybe we had a chance at beating Bryce after all.

"It's a bird. It's a plane. It's the *Fireball!*" said Roger.

"Look out, Superman!" added T. J.

"WOO-HOO!" Roger whooped.

But a minute later we hit the water with a thud.

"Tartar sauce!" I steered around Whale Rock and headed back.

"What happened?" asked Roger.

"I forgot to back the throttle off once we were on plane." That wouldn't happen next time.

"Don't sweat it, dude. Hey, Teej, can I have some of that Laffy Taffy?"

"You're not supposed to be carrying extra snacks," I said.

"Laffy Taffy weighs almost nothing," said Roger. "Hey, I don't like banana, Teej. I want sour apple."

"Three minutes, twenty-three seconds," said Mi as we pulled up to the dock.

THUMP! Something fell out of T. J.'s shirt and hit the deck. He bent to grab it, but not before we saw what it was.

"Coconut water!" I yelled. "T. J., we said no snacks. No extra weight."

"It was just a small bottle," said T. J. "In case I got *dirated*."

"Dehydrated," I said. "Which can only happen if you are without water for more than twenty-four hours, which is in no way going to happen, since we are not going to be on board this boat for an entire day and night!"

"What else you got in there, Mahoney?" Roger tackled T. J. and started pulling on his pants.

"Don't pants me!" T. J. held up his hands. "I surrender!" He hates being pantsed. It's his older brother Mickey's favorite way to get him to do what he wants. It's even more embarrassing if you're wearing dinosaur boxers. Roger wouldn't have done it, but just the threat of it was enough to get T. J. to cave.

T. J. got to his feet and pulled a juice box out of his other pocket, along with a mini box of Cap'n Crunch, three Fruit Roll-Ups, and a jumbo-sized bag of pretzel rods.

"Dude, you're like a magician pulling rabbits out of a hat," said Mi, tapping his pencil on his clipboard. "I had no clue you were a human snack shop."

"Can I have a Fruit Roll-Up?" asked Si.

"What flavor?"

"Give him all of them!" I said. "And get back in the boat."

"Aye, aye, captain!" Roger saluted me.

"Ready . . . set . . . go!" Mi clicked the stopwatch.

Off we went in a surge of spray—again. And again. And again.

# FIRST ONE TO GET LOST WINS!

Every day that week, we practiced getting the *Fireball* to plane. Mi and Si even came to help when they weren't selling clams. We did everything we could think of to lighten the weight to make the boat go fast and help raise the bow. We took out the forward seat and eliminated most of the stuff in the Bug Patrol backpack except the flashlight and some Band-Aids. T. J. brought only small, lightweight snacks, like raisins and beef jerky, the kind of dried-up food astronauts take to the moon so it won't weigh down a rocket when it's in space in zero gravity. It all helped get us up on plane—especially if the wind was going our way and the water was calm.

I couldn't believe the race was less than a week away. I was so excited I kept waking up at sunrise and biking over to the Captain's to sand the *Fireball*'s deck again or check and see that the Seagull's fuel tap was working right. The Captain told me to deep-six (that's Navy slang for throw overboard) my nervousness or I'd end up in a SNAFU for sure. WILCO, I told him (that means "will comply"—wilco, get it?).

That morning Roger, T. J., and I were heading back from making a run around the Point.

"Guys, I need to . . ." T. J.'s voice trailed off and he shrugged.

"Need to what?"

"You know?"

"What? Learn how to weave snowshoes? Turn Bryce Billings into a droid?"

"Visit the facilities," said T. J.

*"Facilities?"* Roger and I looked at him.

"My mom is making us work on our manners," said T. J. "Saying 'bathroom' is rude for some reason."

We approached the marina and I slowed down. I pulled up at the dock and T. J. hopped out while Roger and I tied up the *Fireball*.

"Tell me that is not Bryce and Trippy," I said.

**ZERO GRAVITY**

This means no gravity, or weightlessness. It's what astronauts call it when they float around in a space shuttle, although because they orbit Earth, they are still technically subject to gravity. The space shuttle moves sideways quickly at the same time that it is free-falling to Earth, causing zero gravity, which is why astronauts float around.

"That's not Bryce and Trippy. . . except it is Bryce and Trippy," said Roger. "Contact in three-two-o—"

"So, which one of you clam diggers am I going to have to beat?" said Bryce.

"What are you talking about?" I asked.

"Only one racer is allowed per boat," said Bryce. "It's some dumb new rule."

"For safety," said Trippy, pointing behind us. "It's all in that sign."

Roger and I walked over to the sign. Sure enough, in big black letters it read: ONLY ONE RACER PER BOAT. NO EXCEPTIONS—BOATING SAFETY COMMITTEE. All the other rules were still the same: All racers had to wear PFDs and be able to swim a hundred meters in light clothing, good sportsmanship was mandatory, each boat must be in good working order with a full fuel tank, and no boat could interfere with another boat by cutting into its lane.

"Snap!"

"Why would they do that?" I asked.

Bryce and Trippy rolled their eyes. "Because of that dumb kid who fell out of his cheesy boat last year. He wasn't even in our division."

"Oh."

Roger and I looked at each other. We both remembered when Colum Osborn, Two O's cousin, fell out of Two O's brother Tucker's boat. There were three of them in a nine-foot Alumacraft with a tiller steer motor, you know, one of those little ones in the back. It's a small boat, and they were all big kids.

"Like I said, only good boats and good racers should be allowed in the Classic," sneered Bryce.

"Good boats and good racers have nothing to do with it," said Mr. Blue, the marina manager, who had just come out of the marina office. "This is all about safety. The Classic judges and the Boating Safety Committee agreed unanimously on the one-racer rule. That includes your father, Bryce."

Bryce's mouth dropped open, but no words came out. Roger and I looked at each other. We didn't know Mr. Billings was on the Boating Safety Committee and a judge this year.

"All the other rules are the same," said Mr. Blue. "The one-racer rule is the only new one."

"What are we going to do?" I said, turning to Roger.

"Dude, as if that's a question," said Roger. "Sure, it would have been fun, especially to beat Billings over there." He winked at Bryce, who blew out an annoyed puff of air and rolled his eyes. "But this is your race."

Just then T. J. came running up, waving his arms wildly. His face was red and he was breathing hard.

"What's the matter?" asked Bryce. "Someone steal your lunch?"

Trippy laughed and high-fived Bryce.

"There's this new rule that only one racer is—"

"We know!" we all said.

Roger and T. J. looked at me.

"The *Fireball* will plane easier without us, right, Fish?" T. J. said.

"Absotively posolutely," agreed Roger. "And Teej and I will be with you in spirit every step—or should I say wave— of the way."

"You're starting to sound like Uncle Norman's girlfriend, Venus," I said. Venus Star is an astrologer and she's super nice, but she has some pretty wacky ideas.

The five of us started walking along the dock, heading back to our boats. The *Fireball* was just ahead of us. The *Viper* was tied up on the other end.

"I'm still going to beat you, Finelli," said Bryce.

"Given," said Trippy.

"Oh, yeah?" I said. "I don't think so."

"Of course I will," said Bryce, pointing to the Seagull. "That freaky little motor is no match for my Mercury."

"Is so," I said. "And it's not freaky, it's British, and it was used to power light assault—"

"You think your motor's so great," said Bryce. "Let's race right now."

The word "Okay" was on my lips, but then I remembered listening to the weather forecast that morning. There was the chance of an afternoon thunderstorm, so Uncle Norman and my dad decided to get an early start on their plumbing job, since they don't like to work on outside pipes in the rain.

"I don't know if that's a good idea," I said, thinking about how Uncle Norman always says the biggest danger on a boat is the weather.

Roger and T. J. looked at me in surprise.

"It's not that I don't want to race you or anything," I said quickly. "But it might storm later."

We all looked up at the sky. There were a few clouds, but the sky was blue and the sun was shining.

"You're just scared," said Bryce.

"Am not," I said.

"Are so," Trippy added.

"If you're not, then like I said, let's race right now. Trippy and me against you and Roger and T. J."

T. J. and Roger looked at me again. Racing against Bryce and Trippy was a bad idea for so many reasons. First, there was the weather. Then there was the fact that the marine safety course made it very clear that none of us was supposed to race one another without supervision, *ever*. On top of that, I was the OOD, the officer of the deck, as the Captain would say, and the safety of my men—in this case, Rog and Teej—was my responsibility.

"Hah! I knew you were too scared."

"No, we're not," I said.

"You should be," said Bryce. "You're going to get smoked."

The tips of my ears started getting hot and all thoughts of marine safety flew out of my head. I was sick and tired of

Bryce acting like such a big shot, as if he was better than we were, and thinking he could push us around. It made me so mad, my whole face was burning. Maybe if we beat him, he would finally leave us alone.

"You're the ones who are going to get smoked," I said. "We'll race you right now."

Roger raised his eyebrows and T. J. stopped chewing on one of the carrots his mom was making him eat after she discovered his stash of junk food.

"Deal," said Bryce.

Trippy, a sneaky grin on his face, whispered something to Bryce. The two of them high-fived.

"First one to Get Lost wins."

T. J.'s eyes widened. Roger and I exchanged uneasy glances. "Get Lost Island?"

"That's right, Get Lost Island. If you're not too chicken, and you don't get lost!"

# HOLY SMOKES!
# WE SMOKED THEM!

We piled into the boat. All three of us looked up at the same time. Puffy white clouds floated across the sky.

"You sure it's not going to storm till later?" asked T. J.

"If it storms at all," I said. "We'll be back way before then, anyway." I snuck another glance up at the sky. Were the clouds getting darker, or was that just my imagination?

"If we don't *get lost*," said T. J. "Imagine, years later our skeletons are found, with our scalps all dried up and hanging from a tree."

"That's just a story about those kids who disappeared," said Roger. "And they weren't scalped or anything. You're making that up."

The legend of Get Lost started during World War II. Some kids went there to go fishing and they never came back and their boat was never found. I'm pretty sure grown-ups made it all up so kids back then would stay close to home. See, the grown-ups were afraid the kids would be captured by German saboteurs (spies who try to destroy a country from the inside), because some Nazi spies really did sail from a secret German base and land a U-boat on a beach right in our town. They brought a ton of explosives with them. Their mission was to slow down America's war effort by blowing up stuff like an aluminum company and a railway, and make us so afraid, we would stop fighting. The operation failed and the saboteurs got caught by the FBI, but still, the grown-ups didn't want kids messing around in the water too far from home, in case the Germans tried to do it again.

"Bones were never found," I said, wrapping the pull cord and yanking on the rope to start the engine. "And no boat. There's no evidence it ever happened."

"Did so. Mickey said. No one in town wants us to know the truth. He got it from Burt Babinski, who knows all kinds of secret stuff, like how to use a Taser, 'cause of his dad being chief of police."

"Burt Babinski also said the Porta Potty on the baseball field is a time machine," I said.

"Um, excuse me, coach, I'm just going to help George Washington fight the Redcoats before they slay us and take Long Island for the British," said Roger. "Then I'll be right back to cover left field."

"You never know," said T. J. "Have you ever been in that Porta Potty?"

"No way!" I said, checking that the fuel tank was still close to three-quarters full.

"It stinks!" said Roger.

T. J. nodded. "Exactly."

Just then we heard the hum of a motor as Bryce and Trippy approached. The *Viper* idled up beside us.

"Ready, losers?" Bryce's gold aviator sunglasses glinted in the sun.

"We were born ready," I said, putting on the mirrored sunglasses I had won off him after our first bet. I did it on purpose, because I knew it made him mad.

Bryce looked over the top of his frames and gave me his "You are a cockroach and I'm about to flatten you" look. I looked back at him over my glasses, meeting his stare.

"First one to Get Lost wins," said Roger.

"On your marks . . ." said Bryce.

"Get set . . ." I said.

"Go!"

VROOOOOMMMM!

Bryce and I revved our motors. I did it to check that the Seagull was running well, and to show him his Mercury motor didn't scare me.

"Get ready, guys!" I said.

T. J. sat criss-cross applesauce in the middle of the boat and Roger moved behind me to the stern. I pulled out the throttle and we took off, but the *Viper* shot ahead of us. I pulled the throttle all the way out and the *Fireball* surged forward. We were three boat lengths behind the *Viper*, then two, then just half a boat length. Come on, *Fireball*!

Seconds later, we had caught up. Our two boats raced neck and neck across the bay, our bows lined up, neither one a fraction of an inch ahead of the other. Eli had done a great job with the Seagull. The horsepower was definitely pushing ten if we were able to keep up with Bryce's 9.9 horsepower Mercury.

"Get us on plane, Fish!" said Roger over the engine noise.

We had to get on plane if we wanted to get ahead of the *Viper*. I could feel there was a slight drag pulling us down. I pushed back on the throttle so we dropped back slightly.

**HORSEPOWER**

Invented by Scottish engineer James Watt (1736–1819). When he was working on the steam engine, he wanted to show how fast it was compared to a horse. He calculated the power it took a horse to lift 33,000 pounds one foot in one minute. That is one horsepower.

"Move toward the bow, T. J.!" I shouted. "Roger, lean forward."

Then I smoothly but speedily pulled out the throttle again.

WHOOOOOSSHH!

The *Fireball* got up on plane and shot ahead of the *Viper*. I made sure to pull back on the throttle just enough so we wouldn't fall off. I looked over my shoulder and saw Trippy move aft. Bryce pulled out the throttle.

WHOOSH! The *Viper* got up on plane and zoomed toward us. The next thing I knew, Bryce was steering straight for our bow. Oh, man! He was going to cut us off.

I swerved out of the way just in time as the *Viper* flew past.

PHWOMP! The *Fireball* hit the water.

"Cheaters!" shouted Roger.

"Losers!" Bryce and Trippy's voices floated back to us.

"We have to plane!" Roger said.

I pulled out the throttle and we picked up speed again. The *Viper* was fifty yards or so away. We could still catch them so long as we got up on plane, but we were dragging again. The wind had picked up behind us, which was good. We needed to lighten the load in the back even more to take advantage of it.

"Move forward, Rog. Move back, Teej."

Roger squashed himself into the space next to me. I pulled the backpack out from under the seat. I threw it to T. J. He caught it and leaned forward. It must have lightened the weight enough so the stern wasn't pulled down by the force of water rushing under the boat, because the bow rose and we got up on plane. The wind really helped, and so did the current, which was going our way, too.

"WOO-HOO!" T. J. and Roger high-fived each other.

I focused on the *Viper*. We surged forward, gaining on Bryce and Trippy. Up ahead I could see Lyons Island, where we had found the treasure that turned out to be Captain Kidd's long underwear. Get Lost was about three nautical miles northwest of Lyons Island, but we couldn't take the direct route. It was too close to where the ocean currents flowed into the bay. Those currents were strong and unpredictable, moving the sand around to form shoals, or sandbars, that were hard to see. We needed to go east and take the long way around Lyons Island through Lyons Bay.

"Get 'em, Fish!" shouted Roger.

"Yeah!" shouted T. J., pouring Pop Rocks into his mouth. He must have snuck them, because they were certainly not on his mom's list of healthy snacks. I don't know how he could eat so many without his stomach exploding. Then again, he could eat fifteen fireballs at once. We had named the boat the *Fireball* on account of how all those partly chewed fireballs fell out of T. J.'s mouth onto Captain Kidd's trunk when we found the buried treasure.

We were closing the distance. The *Viper* was now thirty yards ahead of us.

Then twenty.

My heart was pounding so hard I could hear it in my ears. I leaned forward, excited, urging the *Fireball* to go faster. We were going to beat Bryce Billings. Finally, he was going to get what he deserved.

I gripped the steering wheel tighter, keeping my eyes trained straight ahead. Eyes on the prize. Bryce must have felt us gaining on him, because he turned around and looked at me. He made the L sign with his thumb and forefinger.

Then ten.

"You're going to get smoked!" said Roger, waving his fist at the *Viper*.

"You mean YOU'RE going to get smoked!" Trippy hollered back.

Suddenly, Bryce swerved to the left, toward the old buoy. What was he doing? Was he crazy? Didn't he know about the currents and the sandbars? Sure, it was the shortest way to Get Lost, but if you ran into a sandbar you could wreck your boat.

I thought about what Uncle Norman told me when I first got the *Fireball* about the importance of taking a minute to make a good decision on a boat, especially when there were other people involved. Then I thought about how good it would feel to beat Bryce.

My fingers itched to turn left and follow Bryce, but I kept to the right. We headed the opposite direction of the *Viper*.

"They're getting way ahead of us!"

"I know."

"This is the long way."

"I know."

"We're going to lose."

"Not necessarily," I said as we zoomed around Lyons Island. "Not if Bryce and Trippy get the *Viper* stuck in a sandbar."

Roger gave me the thumbs-up.

"Why are there sandbars that way and not this way?" asked T. J., pouring more Pop Rocks into his mouth.

"The currents on that side come right from the ocean. That means those currents are stronger, more like the ocean's currents, and always shifting, which is what creates sandbars. So, there you are, zooming along in your boat, no problem, until WHAM! You hit a sandbar and get stuck. This is the bay side, so the currents aren't so strong and there are no shoals or sandbars."

"Think Bryce knows that?"

I shrugged. He was probably halfway to Get Lost already.

I steered around the end of Lyons Island, past the thick groves of pine and cypress trees. It's a private island owned by Eugenia Lyons, and ever since we found Captain Kidd's long underwear and stuff, it's also a national historic landmark. See, it's been in the Lyons' family since the Montaukett Indians gave it to the first Lyonses almost three hundred years ago. It's also the home of the osprey, or sea hawk, a bird that used to be endangered.

We could see Get Lost off in the distance. Bryce would probably be there in minutes, and beat us by a mile. Get Lost started growing larger as the seconds passed.

As we got closer, T. J. asked, "Where are Bryce and Trippy?"

I was wondering the same thing. They should have been here already.

Get Lost loomed just ahead. I could see the dead brown branches hanging off the trees and the dried-up dune grass in patches across the sand. Suddenly, it seemed awfully quiet. We looked at each other. Even though I knew that story about the kids who disappeared wasn't true, my heart beat faster.

"Holy smokes, dude! We smoked them!" said Roger.

"Unless they docked on the other side," I said. "Maybe they want to pop out and scare us or something."

"Or maybe they got stuck in a sandbar," said Roger.

I slowed the engine as we got closer. There was no one around and we hadn't passed any other boaters on our way. It was pretty gloomy. It didn't help that the sun had disappeared behind a bank of gray clouds. The sky was still blue, but only in a few patches. And the clouds weren't that pale gray that's almost white; they were that darker gray, like the color of a shark's fin. They looked kind of like storm clouds. I sure hoped they weren't planning to act like storm clouds anytime soon.

"Or maybe Bryce and Trippy disappeared like those kids." T. J. shoved more Pop Rocks in his mouth, his face a little pale. "I feel sort of funny—"

"Who wouldn't feel funny after all those Pop Rocks?"

BANG!

"What was that?" asked Roger.

"It sounded like a gun," said T. J., eyes wide.

BANG!

"Maybe one of those German secret agents is still on Get Lost Island and he's shooting at us," whispered T. J., his eyes so wide we could see the whites all around.

"We don't know if it's really a gun," I said, staring to the left. "Anyway, the sound is coming from the other way."

I strained my eyes looking, but I couldn't see anything. I didn't want to tell T. J. it sounded like a gun to me, too. The wind picked up just then, gusting across the water. Waves rocked the *Fireball* from side to side. Something that sounded like a voice seemed to be calling out on the wind.

"Help!" I thought I heard the voice say.

"Did you hear that?" Roger asked.

"What?" asked T. J.

"I thought I heard someone say 'Help.'"

"Me too," I said, a shiver running up my spine.

"Oh, jeepo!" said T. J. "Someone got shot!"

"Help!" The word came more clearly as the wind died down.

"I think you might be right, Teej," said Roger, talking fast the way he does when he's nervous. "I hope you're wrong. Yes, I hope wrong is right, that is—"

BANG!

I turned the boat to the left.

"What are you doing?" asked Roger.

"It's the first law of boating, to help someone in trouble. So if Bryce and Trippy need help, it's up to us to help them," I said, trying to sound braver than I felt.

I steered the *Fireball* slowly and carefully around Get Lost. It was getting darker out as any patches of blue disappeared under clouds that seemed to get grayer and heavier with each passing second. They covered the sky, making it harder to see.

I took off Bryce's sunglasses. I didn't want to hit a sand-bar, especially now that we were on the ocean side of the island. "Teej, you look over the port side. Rog, you look over the starboard side," I said.

"What are we looking for?" asked T. J.

"Sandbars," I said.

Roger moved to the right of the boat and T. J. moved to the left, eyes on the water. I maneuvered the *Fireball* slowly over the waves.

Once we got past the trees, we spotted the *Viper*. Bryce was standing in front of the wheel. He had a crazed look on his face. Trippy was slumped beside him.

"Trippy's dead," said T. J.

Bryce pointed his gun right at us.

"Don't shoot!" said Roger.

"I surrender!" T. J. held up his hands.

"Help us!" said Bryce.

Trippy jumped up, yelling, too.

"It's a miracle!" said T. J. "Trippy rose from the dead."

"He was never dead," I said.

"How do you know?"

"That's not a real gun."

"Looks like a gun," said Roger. "Sounds like a gun."

"It's a flare gun."

"We didn't see any flares," said Roger.

"It must be broken," I said, steering the *Fireball* closer. "I don't know what Bryce is doing with it. They're illegal for anyone under eighteen to use."

"It could be a trick," said Roger.

"They are the ones who got tricked by hitting a sandbar."

There was a rumbling sound. We all looked up. The sky had gotten even darker. There was a giant cumulonimbus cloud right above us. That was not a good sign. The cumulonimbus cloud is also known as a thunderhead.

A boat is just about the worst place to be in a thunderstorm. Lightning always strikes the tallest things around, which would be us, since it wasn't like the *Fireball* or the *Viper* had lightning protection systems.

We reached Bryce and Trippy just as the first few drops of rain started to fall.

"What's wrong with your boat? Did you hit a sandbar?" I asked, staring at Bryce, who was standing there, still holding the flare gun. "And put that thing away. It's dangerous."

"I guess. We rammed into something and then the engine just died." He waved the flare gun around. "This thing doesn't even work. I should have taken the other one from my dad's boat."

"You stole it?"

Bryce shrugged. "It's not like my dad would notice or care."

It seemed awfully strange that someone like Mr. Billings, who was on the Boating Safety Commission and a judge for the Classic, wouldn't keep better track of his flare guns. Uncle Norman always knew exactly where all of his boating equipment was, especially anything incendiary (that means able to cause a fire), like a flare gun.

"Are you stuck, or did the propeller break?" I asked.

"The prop broke, I think," said Bryce.

"There was this grinding sound," said Trippy.

"Then the motor stopped working. I gave it a ton of fuel, but it still wouldn't go," said Bryce.

"You probably flooded the engine on top of breaking your prop," I said, shaking my head.

"Whatever," said Bryce. "You need to tow us."

Thunder rumbled again. We had to hurry, because thunder meant lightning wasn't far behind. The sky had gotten even darker.

I tied one end of the rope to the *Fireball* and tossed the other to Bryce. He tied it to the *Viper*'s gunnel.

"Come on!" I said. "Jump!"

Bryce jumped on board, with Trippy right behind him. The rain started to pour.

BOOM! Lightning streaked across the sky.

"AAAUGHHH!!!"

"We have to get out of here!" said Bryce.

I nodded and turned the *Fireball* around. There was only one place to go. Get Lost was our only hope. . . .

# SNAP GOES THE *VIPER!*

Waves rocked the boat. Wind gusted around us. Water splashed over the sides. The coast guard would definitely have a red flag flying. That meant small crafts were not supposed to go out on the water. The *Fireball* was a small craft.

"Hurry, Fish!"

I gripped the wheel so tight my knuckles were white. The chop was really strong, and waves pushed against the boat, making it hard to steer. I squinted through the rain at the green and brown blur that I knew had to be Get Lost.

Just then a huge wave crashed against the boat. Water sloshed over the sides and filled the bottom.

"Bail!" I ordered.

But no one had a bucket to bail with. T. J. took off his hat and used that to toss out some water. The other guys just used their hands. It helped some, but water still sloshed around our ankles.

The next wave knocked hard into the port side. "AAAHHH!" Roger and T. J. slid to starboard and bumped into Bryce and Trippy.

"Look out!"

My hands slipped on the wheel. The boat tipped to the right.

"AAAAHHHHH!"

"Move left!"

I gripped the wheel. Bryce and Roger moved to the left and the boat righted itself. I took a deep breath and made sure we were still going in the correct direction. Get Lost was dead ahead about a hundred yards away. Sea spray stung my eyes, and I had to close them for a second. I had to stay calm and not panic, just like I learned in the marine safety course. I was the OOD. It was up to me to get us all to safety.

Another wave sloshed over the sides. The boys kept on bailing.

"Hurry, Fish!"

The boat floundered. We were moving so slowly it felt like we were a tugboat struggling to pull a steamship. I didn't have to look behind me to know the *Viper* had taken on water. That was why it was so heavy.

## LIGHTNING

It's an electric current formed in a thundercloud in the sky when frozen raindrops collide. The cloud fills up with electrical charges—positive charges (protons) at the top, negative charges (electrons) at the bottom. The negative charges at the bottom of the cloud attract the positive charges of what is sticking up on the ground. When those charges connect—ZAP!—lightning strikes. (The heat of the lightning bolt causes the air to explode with a BOOM, which is thunder.)

If we weren't pulling all that extra weight, we would get to Get Lost a lot faster. At this rate, we would never make it—or worse, we might flip over. Getting trapped under a boat in a storm was how people died.

I couldn't let that happen. There was only one thing to do. I had to cut the rope. But the *Viper* might be history.

Then again, if we didn't get out of this storm, we might be history, too.

Lightning flashed, lighting up the sky with a purple glow. Thunder boomed so loud it felt like it was right over our heads. The biggest wave yet hit us hard on the starboard side. T. J., Roger, Bryce, and Trippy all rolled into one another. The boat listed dangerously to the left.

"AAAHHHH!"

I stuck one hand in my pocket and left the other on the wheel. I felt around for Grandpa Finelli's pocket-knife. It didn't have a knife anymore, but it did have scissors and a spoon.

"We have to cut the line!" I said, waving the scissors at the guys.

"What?!" said Bryce, scrambling to his feet.

"The line! We have to cut the line if we want to get out of here. Grab the wheel."

"No way!" Bryce yelled.

"I have to," I said. "Otherwise we'll never make it to Get Lost."

Lightning lit up the sky purple-white again. Rain poured down all around us.

"We can't just leave my boat," said Bryce, pushing his wet hair out of his eyes to glare at me. "It'll get wrecked!"

Thunder boomed again and waves rocked the boat.

"Hurry up!" said Roger, huddling on the bench to try and stay dry in the downpour.

"Somebody grab the wheel!" I said.

"Don't cut the rope!" Bryce said, lunging for my left hand, which was holding the scissors. "My dad will kill me if anything happens to my boat."

"Something already did happen," I said, just as another wave rocked the boat.

Bryce slid backward across the deck, away from me and into T. J. and Roger. I shoved the knife in my pocket and grabbed the wheel with both hands to steady it. Trippy was just behind me. Another streak of lightning forked across the sky. It was so close, I could practically feel the electricity buzzing through me.

"Take the wheel!" I ordered Trippy. "Keep it straight for Get Lost. Okay?"

Trippy stared at me dumbly, his face as white as the bright-white hull of the *Fireball*.

I turned around and bent down, feeling for the rope. The rain was coming down in sheets. I had to keep rubbing my eyes to get the water out of them so I could see. The rope was wet and slippery and hard to hold. More waves rocked the boat.

"Hurry, Fish!"

I pulled the knife out of my pocket, and squeezed the scissor blades together with as much force as I could. Nothing happened. The boat started to spin. I turned around. Trippy had let go of the wheel!

"Hold the wheel!" I yelled into the wind.

No one else said a word. Not even Bryce, who looked just as scared now as the other guys.

"It's too wet!" screamed Trippy.

"You can do it! Just grab the wheel."

He finally did and the boat stopped spinning. I had to cut the rope fast before Trippy lost total control again.

I bent down and snapped the scissors back and forth. They slipped out of my hands. I lunged and grabbed them. I sawed at the rope with one of the scissor blades as hard as I could. A few strands popped off. I kept sawing away. More strands popped off. It helped that the rope was one of the Captain's oldest.

SNAP!

The *Viper* listed to the starboard side, the roll bar tipping dangerously close to the water. Waves rocked into it from the port side. The *Viper* shot up as the *Fireball* started to spin. Then the *Viper* bounced over the waves away from us.

I didn't waste another second. I pushed Trippy over and grabbed the wheel from him. He had a dazed look on his face. All the guys did, especially Bryce, as he watched his boat disappear into the storm. . . .

# TUNA EYEBALLS ON TOAST. YUM! YUM!

I revved the engine and we surged forward. We were moving at last! Get Lost was getting closer. I held on tight to the wheel as another gust of wind and rain hit us from the starboard side. We listed to port, but I turned the wheel fast to straighten us out. Come on, *Fireball*!

We surged forward. Another twenty yards and we would reach the beach.

My heart stopped beating quite as fast. Fifteen yards. Then ten. Five. Close enough.

"Let's go!" I said. "Help me beach the boat."

Everybody hopped into the water. We sloshed through waves and driving rain and pulled and pushed the *Fireball* onto the shore. We were soaking wet and shivering.

The five of us huddled together under a canopy of trees as the storm raged around us. Bryce sat a little bit away from us, as far as he could get from me. He kept shooting me evil glares, like a viperfish (no kidding—it's one of the meanest-looking sea creatures you ever saw), but I didn't care. I couldn't stop thinking about what T. J. had said about Get Lost and the kids who disappeared. It was so dark and gloomy, I suddenly started feeling like maybe the story was true after all.

"I wish it wasn't so dark," said T. J., as if he was reading my mind.

"A little light would be nice," I agreed, sneaking a peek over my shoulder at the shadowy trees behind us.

"Light coming right up." Roger opened the Bug Patrol backpack, which he had remembered to take from the boat, and pulled something from it. "Da-da-da-da!"

"Oooh, a Barbie flashlight!" said Bryce.

"Hey, you want light or not?"

We all nodded as Roger flipped the switch. A thin beam of light shot out and then died. He knocked it against his leg and flipped the switch again. Nothing.

"Barbie, you light up my life! Come back to me!"

Everyone laughed except for Bryce.

"Let me try," I said. Roger tossed me the flashlight. I popped out the batteries, put them back in, and screwed on the end again. Then I flicked the switch. A beam of light shot out. We held our breath, wondering if it would flicker out again. A few more seconds passed.

"Barbie, you rock!" joked Roger, as I tossed the flashlight back to him.

We all smiled. It wasn't much, but there was something reassuring about that little light in the great big gloom of Get Lost.

Roger put the flashlight in the middle of the uneven circle we had made under the trees.

"Hey, it's like a campfire," said Roger, pretending to warm his hands over the light.

"Where are the s'mores?" asked Trippy.

Again, we all laughed except for Bryce. "This isn't funny, you know. My boat is wrecked and lost—"

"No, Billings, *we're* lost, as in on Get Lost. The *Viper* didn't get to Get Lost. Get it?" Roger's brown eyes glowed in the light. There's nothing he loves more than wordplay.

"My dad is going to kill me," said Bryce. "How can you laugh at a time like this?"

"I'm sorry, dude," said Trippy, glancing uneasily at his friend.

"We had no choice, Billings," I said. "We wouldn't have made it otherwise. We had to get out of the storm. I'm sure he'll understand that."

Another crack of thunder sounded over our heads. Seconds later lightning flashed again.

"See what I mean?"

"I thought we were going to die," said Trippy, shivering. Roger and T. J. nodded.

Bryce hung his head. "You don't get it. None of you do. My dad is going to kill me. It's always me. Beck never messes anything up. All I ever hear about is how perfect my brother is, and how come I can't be like him. Beck never wrecked a boat, that's for sure."

Beck Billings was in seventh grade and a football and lacrosse star. He was also the number-one student in his grade and a great pianist. Everyone loved Beck, including Summer, Roger's older sister, who had a major crush on him.

The thing was, Beck was a nice guy. He wasn't stuck up at all. I actually started feeling bad for Bryce that his dad would compare him to his brother all the time. Nobody could compete with Beck. It had to be rough.

"Look on the bright side, Billings," said Roger as lightning forked across the sky. "I'm sure your dad would rather you were alive than turned into Billings flambé by a bolt of lightning."

"Funny, Huckleton," said Bryce. "The bottom line is if it wasn't for Fish cutting the *Viper* loose, I wouldn't be in this mess."

"What?!"

"The truth is you should be thanking him for saving all of us," said Roger.

Trippy nodded at me and mouthed "Thank you" so I could see but Bryce couldn't.

"Without Fish we would be fish food, shark bait, whale chow," said Roger.

"You know what this means?" said T. J. all of a sudden. "We won."

"Hey, that's right," said Roger. "We beat you, Billings."

"No, you didn't," said Bryce. "We had an accident. It doesn't count."

"Yes, it does. It's like the Indy Five Hundred. Just because some cars get wrecked or burn up, the first car to cross the finish line wins."

"You said the first one to Get Lost wins," I said. "And we were the first ones."

"We won fair and square," said Roger. "Come on. Say it."

"Whatever," said Bryce. "So you won. Who cares? All that matters is my boat is lost somewhere in that storm and it's wrecked and it's all your fault, Fish Finelli!"

"How is that *my* fault?" I said. "You're the one who got stuck in a sandbar and broke your prop."

"So? You still didn't have to cut the rope. I'll never forgive you for that."

If I felt bad for Bryce before because of how his dad treated him, all my feelings of sympathy were flambéed right out of me. How dare he blame me?

Roger must have seen the angry look on my face, because before I could start yelling at Bryce, he said, "How about a game? It will serve two wonderful purposes: to take our minds off our terrible fate and to warm us up." He rubbed his arms.

"Now that you mention it, I'm freezing," said Trippy, pulling his shorts down over his knees.

I was cold, too. There were goose bumps up and down my arms.

"What kind of game?" asked Trippy.

"Don't Hesitate is always fun," said T. J., whose teeth had started chattering like those plastic windup teeth you buy on Halloween.

"Only if I get to pick the category," said Roger.

"Animals," suggested T. J.

"*Bor*-ing," said Roger.

"Dinosaurs," said Trippy.

Interesting, I thought. I remembered Trippy dressing up as a T. rex back when he and Bryce were in first grade and we were in kindergarten, when we were all friends. Back then we all used to play hide-and-seek and dodgeball and stuff at recess. Then Trippy and Bryce went to surf camp the summer after third grade. After that, they started dressing different and acting different and Bryce started being the big bully he is now. And Trippy went along with it and stopped being friends with us, too.

"Nah," said Bryce, back to being his usual, bossy self. "Dinosaurs have too many long, weird names."

"I've got it!" said Roger. "Nasty-wasty, ucky-yucky lunches provided by the Whooping Hollow Elementary School!"

We all looked at one another. No one knew what to say.

"I take that as a yes," said Roger. "Don't Hesitate, the subject is nasty-wasty, ucky-yucky lunches, starting with greasy, grimy, gopher-gut tacos, kidney beans, and dog hair."

"Nasty," I said.

"Wasty," said T. J.

"Your turn, Fish."

"Ground-up chicken feet salad on a moldy bun with wasp crackers," I said.

"T. J.?"

"Tuna eyeballs on toast with pickled grasshoppers and bird's nest soup."

"Yum! Yum!" said Roger. "Bryce?"

All eyes turned to Bryce. "Egg puke on whole wheat, with french-fried worm soup."

"Totally gross, Billings! Excellent!"

Bryce glared at Roger, who was busy pointing at Trippy.

Trippy frowned, concentrating. "Fried spiders with rice . . . um . . . raccoon snot . . ."

"You hesitated!" said Roger.

"I did?"

"Yes, before you said raccoon snot."

Before we could start another round, T. J., whose favorite subject was always food, said, "You know, fried spiders, especially tarantulas, are a delicacy in Japan."

"Gross!"

"How do you know that?" I asked.

"From *Eating Adventures Around the World*," said T. J. "It's a cooking show. You know, in some countries they eat monkey brains and goat brains."

"EWWWWW!!!!"

"I'm hungry," said Trippy just as my stomach rumbled.

"Hungry enough to eat monkey brains?"

Everyone laughed.

Roger and I looked at T. J.

"What?" T. J. asked.

"What you got?"

"Not a lot," said T. J. "On account of the weight restrictions on the boat."

"You have food?" said Bryce.

T. J. nodded. We all watched as he reached into his pocket and pulled out a handful of Jolly Ranchers. He laid them out in front of him. This was followed by a crushed-up bag of Goldfish crackers, a pair of wax lips, and a small box of Craisins.

We all looked at the pile of snacks.

"I want the wax lips," said Bryce.

"Me too," said Trippy. "I'm real thirsty."

"Me three," said Roger.

"Looks like it's time for the Jolly Rancher Challenge," said T. J. "Whoever wins gets the lips, and then we share the rest. Deal?"

"What's the Jolly Rancher Challenge?"

"Whoever can unwrap a Jolly Rancher fastest in his mouth, using only his teeth and his tongue, wins."

T. J. smiled. He always wins the Jolly Rancher Challenge. Maybe because he's the one who made it up in the first place.

T. J. handed out the Jolly Ranchers. "Everybody ready?"

We all nodded, even Bryce.

"On your marks . . . get set . . . go!"

We popped the candies in our mouths and started biting and sucking on them. We must have looked pretty crazy. T. J. won, of course, but Trippy was only a few seconds behind him. Trippy told us about this one time he ate ten fluffer-nutter sandwiches and then threw up in his mother's prize rosebushes. The candy must have put Bryce in a better

mood, because he told us how he ate a dog biscuit on a dare and it was kind of tasty. We all laughed, including him.

We were so busy eating the rest of the snacks that we didn't notice that the rain had slowed to a drizzle and the wind had died down.

"Hey, guys, look!" said T. J., pointing to where a thin trickle of sunlight poked out of the clouds.

The water had calmed down, too. As we got to our feet, the sun came out for real, lighting up the gloom. Get Lost didn't look nearly so spooky anymore.

"Looks like we're good to go," I said.

We all piled into the *Fireball*.

"We better find my boat, Finelli," said Bryce, frowning and waving a finger in my face. All traces of his good mood were long gone.

"Take a chill pill, Billings," said Roger.

"A, B, C, D, E, F, G . . ." I started saying the alphabet to myself to keep my temper from rising, just like the first Roman emperor, Caesar Augustus. That's how he kept himself calm when he started getting mad, and why he was known as a wise ruler. I wasn't an emperor, but I was the OOD. I had to be calm to take care of my boat and my men.

**CAESAR AUGUSTUS
(63 BC–AD 14)**

The first emperor of the Roman Empire, he ruled from 31 BC to 14 AD. He expanded the borders of Rome, adding Egypt, parts of Africa, and much of Europe to the empire. Wise and strong, he began an era of peace in Rome and built temples, theaters, and roads. The month of August is named after him.

I pulled on the rope to start the Seagull, checking the fuel level. We had less than half a tank, which was just about enough to get us home. I was pretty sure the *Viper* hadn't sunk, because whalers are pretty much unsinkable, but less than half a tank of fuel was not enough to go chasing after it if it had drifted too far away. All I could do was hope it was close by as I pulled out the throttle and we headed away from the island.

We had only gone a little ways when what do you know? We saw a white shape bobbing on the waves with a telltale green stripe on the side.

PHEW!

"See, your boat is fine," said Roger.

I cut the engine and we drifted closer to inspect the damage. The *Viper* was fine, as in it was in one piece, but it was definitely listing to starboard from all the water in the bottom. Plus, it wasn't like it was going to run with a broken prop. I revved the engine.

"Where's the line?" asked Bryce. "You need to tie it to your boat."

I shook my head.

"What?!"

"It's too heavy for the *Fireball* to pull with all the weight we already have," I said. "We'll never make it. We don't have enough gas."

"You're just saying that so my boat gets more messed up, and then you'll be able to beat me in the Classic," said Bryce, frowning.

"This has nothing to do with the Classic," I said. "It's about safety. You need to come back in a bigger boat with a bigger engine to pull a load that heavy. Don't you remember the section in the Marine Safety Course about weight restrictions and the ratio of—"

"You think you're so smart, Fish Finelli," sneered Bryce. "Just get us out of here, so I can go get my boat. I'm never going to forget what you did. Get ready to get clobbered at the Classic, loser!"

# HUNG, DRAWN,
# AND GROUNDED!

"You're grounded, young man," my dad told me as he paced in front of the piano bench in our living room, where I was sitting. I felt like he was Darth Vader and I was Luke Skywalker, and he was about to blast me off the Death Star and into outer space.

"Aw, Dad," I said in a very un-Luke Skywalker way. Then again, I didn't have a light saber to defend myself.

Shrimp put his gigantic head down on my feet. He let out a sad, doggy whine and slobbered all over my toes. I couldn't believe after everything I had been through, I was grounded on top of it.

I confessed all the details to my parents when I got home. It turns out the Captain had called during the storm when he didn't see the *Fireball* at the dock. That worried my mom, so she called my dad and Roger's and T. J.'s moms. Nobody knew where any of us were.

I explained about Bryce and the storm and Get Lost, figuring honesty is always the best policy and since everything had turned out okay—except for the *Viper* getting messed up—all was well that ended well. My dad didn't see it that way, though.

"Do you want to go over it again?" My dad ticked off each of my crimes. "One, you went to a dangerous place without permission. Two, you did not tell anyone where you were going. Three, you were irresponsible about the weather. Four, you endangered not just yourself, but your friends. Am I forgetting anything?"

I kept quiet. I knew that was one of those trick questions that adults ask, but they don't really want you to answer. If you do, things will pretty much only go from nasty to wasty.

"He did rescue Bryce and Trippy," said my mom.

"Hmm . . ."

"He did get everyone safely to shore."

"Hmm . . ."

"He did act in a calm and courageous manner."

"Hmm . . ."

Wow! I sounded like a real hero, like Luke Skywalker. Maybe they would go easy on me.

THUMP! THUMP! Shrimp wagged his tail. He must have thought I sounded like a real hero, too.

My parents stepped into the hall to decide my sentence. I played the first few measures of "Für Elise" on the piano while I waited. It's my dad's favorite. I figured it might help.

"Your father and I agreed you are grounded for one week, starting now," my mom said, walking into the room.

"A whole week?! What about the race?" That was on Saturday, exactly six days away.

"You better forget the race," said my mom. "You're going to be racing around here doing chores for me, mister."

**"Für Elise"**
Bagatelle No. 25 in A Minor, known as "Für Elise" (that means "For Elise" in German). It was composed by Ludwig von Beethoven around 1810 and published in 1867. It is still a mystery who Elise was.

"But, Mom . . ."

"Don't 'But, Mom' me. It's only a week. Would you like it to be the whole summer?"

This was another one of those trick questions. I sighed, not answering, and kicked my toe against the piano bench leg where a big chunk of wood was missing from when Shrimp chewed it off.

"Does he get to race for good behavior?" asked Uncle Norman, sticking his head in the door.

My parents looked at each other.

"If he does absolutely everything you ask him to do, and he waxes my motorcycle, too?" Uncle Norman winked at me.

Like I said, Uncle Norman is the best uncle in the entire world.

My parents looked at each other again.

"Maybe," they said at the same time.

"We better go, Carmine." Uncle Norman turned to my dad. "We have some automatic toilets to install."

"Those work by electric sensors, right?" I asked, grateful for the change in topic.

"Yep," said Uncle Norman, smiling, like he was glad for the change in topic, too. "An electric signal gets sent to the electrical flush valve."

"The first flush toilet was called a water closet and belonged to King Minos of Crete two thousand, eight hundred years ago, right, Dad? Didn't you say it was a great feat of engineering, like so much of plumbing?"

"Not even knowing your plumbing history will get you out of this, grounded boy," said my dad in a gruff voice, but he smiled and ruffled my hair.

I walked out of the room and smack into Feenie and Mmm.

"Busted!" said Feenie.

"Zip it, Feenie."

"T. J. got busted, too," said Mmm. "Also 'cause he ate the whole bowl of lime Jell-O salad with teeny marshmallows my mom made for the Cat Fancy Club Meeting. He has to clean out all the litter boxes, groom all the cats, and straighten out the junk bathtub, and he can't have any dessert till he graduates from middle school."

"No dessert!" Feenie shook her head. "That's really bad."

My first job was to mow the lawn with our very old lawnmower. It's one of those push ones without a motor, so it takes like ten times as long as an electric mower to cut the grass, and requires a whole lot of elbow grease.

I was already sweating as I mowed carefully around my mom's petunias when Roger stuck his head over the

hedge. He had a hose in his hand, but no water was coming out of it.

"What's the verdict?" asked Roger.

"Hung, drawn, and grounded!"

"Likewise."

"Guess being irresponsible in the mind of a parent is as bad as committing high treason against the king, like those guys back in the Middle Ages who got hung, drawn, and quartered."

Roger nodded. "You're telling me, dude. I've got to weed all the flower beds, water every green thing for miles around, take out the garbage, mop the kitchen, sweep the porch, vacuum and dust the whole house, and clean the bathroom with that bleachy bubbly stuff, every single day for an indefinite amount of time."

"Whew!" I said. Roger's mom sure was strict. She was way stricter than his dad. When Roger's dad was around, he used to make her laugh and joke her out of her strictness. He's a joker, just like Roger.

"How long you got?" asked Roger.

"A week."

"What about the race?"

"Only for good behavior."

"The old good behavior routine," said Roger. "It's their secret weapon to make you do everything they want and more."

"I know! Better start watering."

Roger flipped the handle on the hose, but no water came out. He turned the gauge on the nozzle. Still no water. He put his eye up to the nozzle and pressed the handle. All of a sudden, a stream of water shot out and hit him in the face.

"Aaahh!" he yelled, jumping back.

I started laughing.

"RO-ger!!!!" his older sister, Summer, yelled. "Don't forget to be careful with that old hose. Oh, and where is my iced tea?"

"Nice trick with the hose! Get it yourself, Winter!"

"Mom says you have to listen to me, or you're going to be grounded until you start shaving."

Roger held up the hose like it was a sword and he was going to run Summer through with it. I went back to mowing the lawn. I still had more chores to do, like weed the flower beds, sweep the garage, and clean out the grill—and that was just today. I wondered what my parents had planned for the rest of the week.

"Fish, Mom says you have to help Mmm and me fix our magic coach," said Feenie.

She and Mmm waved their magic wands at me. Behind them was a cardboard box that they had colored pink and decorated with sparkles.

"What do you want me to do?"

"Make it go," said Feenie.

"You're the Fapits," I said. "You're the ones with magic powers."

"Better do the princesses' bidding, or they'll turn you into a frog or a puddle of green slime or something!" Roger called over the hedge.

Feenie and Mmm nodded at me.

I sighed.

"Guys!" T. J. came running up to us, a pink plastic bottle in his hand and a pink hairbrush sticking out of his pocket. "Have you seen Champion Tatiana?" he gasped, trying to catch his breath.

"Oh, no!" Roger and I both said.

"I was grooming her and the mousse was next, so I went to get it, and—"

"You have to groom a moose?!" said Roger. "Wow, Teej! And I thought my punishment was bad."

"I don't mean a moose moose, I mean hair mousse," said T. J., holding up the pink bottle. "Fabulous Feline really makes their coats shine, but Champion Tatiana hates it."

Feenie and Mmm looked at each other and started slowly backing away.

MEOW! came from the azalea bush beside Feenie and Mmm's magic coach.

"Aha! That meow sounds like our good friend, Champion Teeter-Totter of Blah-Bu-De-Blah," said Roger, pointing the hose over the hedge at Feenie and Mmm. "She wouldn't happen to be trying to hang a ride in your magic coach?"

"She's our long-lost sister princess who the big bad witch turned into a kitty cat," said Feenie.

"And you can't have her," said Mmm to T. J.

But T. J. was too fast. He had already run over to the carriage and scooped out Champion Tatiana. "I'm in big enough trouble already," he said. "If I don't do her hair all pouffy for the Cat Fancy Club Meeting, I'll never get to have dessert again. See you, guys."

T. J. dashed out of the yard.

"*Ro-ger*, where is my tea?" came Summer's annoyed voice.

"Hey, Rog. Your princess is summoning you now. You better do her bidding."

Roger sighed.

*"Fiiiisssssshhhh!"* came Feenie's and Mmm's voices. "The princesses need you to fix their magic coach *noooowwww.*"

Having princesses for sisters sure made being hung, drawn, and grounded worse torture than it already was. . . .

# READY, SET, KABOOM!

I officially stopped being hung, drawn, and grounded the night before the race. I had done everything my mom and dad asked—even dust-busting under the backseat of the car, where all the crumbs and sand and dog hair and stuff get stuck, and polishing all twenty-one doorknobs inside and outside our house.

I called Roger and T. J. to tell them the news.

"Excellent, dude!" said Roger. "I'm ungrounded, too."

T. J.'s grounding was off also, except he still couldn't have dessert.

I was so excited and nervous I could barely sleep. The next morning, my mom made my favorite breakfast of cinnamon toast and Tang. In case you don't know, Tang is this powdered drink that used to be popular with astronauts

## JOHN GLENN
## (1921–)

On February 20, 1962, Glenn was the first American astronaut to orbit the Earth, on the Mercury-Atlas 6 Mission. His space capsule, *Friendship 7*, circled the globe three times during a flight lasting 4 hours, 55 minutes, and 23 seconds. It was named Mercury after the Roman god of speed and Friendship 7 by John Glenn, to honor his fellow mission members.

in the United States space program. You just add water and stir. I figured if it was good enough for John Glenn to drink on his Mercury mission, it was good enough for me to drink for the Captain Kidd Classic.

Before I ran out the door, my parents hugged me and wished me luck.

"See you at the race!" said my dad.

"Be careful," said my mom.

"Abracadabra!" said Feenie. Then she threw fairy dust all over me.

I was still brushing pink glitter out of my hair when I met Roger and T. J. at the Captain's dock.

"Dude, you look like a Sno Ball."

"Yum!" said T. J. "Those are my favorite cupcakes."

They both tackled me and rubbed my head to get the glitter off.

"Ouch, guys! Come on. We've got to go."

"Better," said Roger, studying my head. "But your hair still looks sort of pink."

We piled into the *Fireball*. It sure drove smooth and fast with the racing fuel Eli gave me. By the time we got to the marina, a crowd had already gathered. I could see my parents, Feenie, Uncle Norman, and Venus. They waved as soon as they spotted us. Mr. and Mrs. Mahoney, Mickey, and Mmm waved, too, and so did Mrs. Huckleton and Summer.

Off to one side, Mi and Si were busy selling clams. The Captain stood next to a rusty old cannon in front of a platform that was the judges' stand. Mr. Billings, Bryce's dad, was sitting there, with Mr. Blue, the marina manager, and Mr. de Quincy, Clementine's dad.

I looked around for Clementine, but I didn't see her anywhere.

"Ready to smoke the competish?!" said Roger.

"Ready to smoke 'em." I pulled the *Fireball* up to the dock.

"You mean, *you're* going to get smoked, Fish," called out Bryce, pulling up next to me.

"Smoked fish. That's what I call a delicacy," said Roger.

T. J. and I laughed. "Good one, dude."

"Whatever, losers," sneered Bryce. "My motor is unstoppable now."

"Why?" I asked.

"Got the biggest, most amazing prop ever," said Bryce. "I had to, after you cut my boat loose and almost ruined it."

"I didn't do anything to your boat," I said, trying not to get mad. "You're the one who wrecked it in the sandbar." I was pretty sure the cotter pin that held the propeller to the engine shaft had snapped off. That was probably why he needed a new prop. Then I remembered what Eli had told me about the danger of big propellers.

Even though I knew Bryce wouldn't listen, I had to say something. "If the diameter and the pitch of the prop make your motor rev too fast, you know it might blow," I said.

"You're just scared, loser!" said Bryce, hopping out of his boat.

"Honest, Bryce, you don't want your engine to blow," I said, but he was already heading over to where his older brother, Beck, was standing with Trippy by the judges' stand. Summer was on Beck's other side, laughing and flipping her long hair around like she always does around Beck. Mr. Blue was in front of the stand, holding a clipboard to sign in the racers.

"Save your breath, Fish," said Roger. "Once a big head, always a big head."

"Have a fireball," said T. J.

He handed one to me and one to Roger, and put an entire fistful in his own mouth. Like I said, I don't know how he can eat so many. I could feel the burn from just one.

"Fireballs for the *Fireball*!" We bumped fists and did our secret handshake.

"I better go register," I said and ran up to the judges' stand.

"Fish Finelli, the *Fireball*, sir," I said. "Race one, Eleven and Under."

"I've got you right here, Mr. Finelli. Good luck." He winked. "Next?"

"Two O," said Two O. "I mean, Owen Osborn. The *Comet*."

Two O and I high-fived and then knocked into each other as someone pushed us from behind.

"True Taylor," said Bryce's friend, the boy from Sandstone Cove. "The *Barracuda*."

Two O and I shook our heads and rolled our eyes at True's back.

"Break a leg, Fish!" Two O called as we headed off the stand.

"You too," I said and pushed my way through the crowd.

"The Captain Kidd Classic will start in exactly seven and a half minutes!" said Mr. Blue through a megaphone. "Racers, to your boats."

I had to hurry. Race One, the youngest class, was always first. When I got back to the *Fireball*, T. J. and Roger were waiting for me.

"Good luck, Fish!"

"*Zhu ni hao yun*, dude!" said Roger.

"Huh?"

"That's 'good luck' in Mandarin. I can't believe you don't know that, Mr. Dictionary."

"Hey, my mom isn't studying Chinese like yours." I grinned. "Thanks, guys."

I watched them walk away. It suddenly struck me that I was going to be racing all by myself. It had always been the three of us—Roger with his cracks, T. J. with his snacks. I got this little lump in my throat for some reason.

"Love the pink hair, loser!" Bryce was back.

"Quit it, would you?" I said, tightening the screws on the Seagull's cylinder one last time.

Just then a kid in a red baseball cap ran up to Bryce. He mumbled something about a Phillips-head screwdriver and a loose carburetor.

Bryce shook his head. "I can't tighten your carburetor. The race is about to start."

The kid bit his lip, looking upset. I watched him walk over to the next boat, the *Barracuda*. It was True's boat, the one with the blue stripe. The kid in the red hat must have asked True the same question and gotten the same answer, because he walked away with his head down.

"Three minutes to go!" Mr. Blue's voice boomed through the megaphone.

The kid in the red hat headed over to a boat with a silver stripe a few boats away from the *Barracuda*. He started fiddling around with his engine, which looked like a brand-new Evinrude and was an awesome motor. It clearly wasn't starting. Next to his boat was the *Comet*, Two O's little Alumacraft, the same one that belonged to his brother, Tucker, that their cousin Colum fell out of at the last Classic. When Two O saw me looking in his direction, he waved and gave me a thumbs-up.

I looked out at the course. It went all the way around the harbor, past the old bell buoy in a semicircle marked off by red buoys. I thought about how the race was about to start and how I had been waiting for this moment for so long. Then I remembered that the first law of boating is to help someone in trouble.

"Two minutes to go!"

I grabbed my Phillips-head screwdriver and ran to the silver boat. It was called the *Zephyr*. So this was the eighth boat.

"I can tighten your carburetor with this," I said, carefully turning first one screw and then the other with the screwdriver to secure them to the carb. "That should do the trick."

The kid in the red hat looked at me in surprise. The hat was so low on his head I could barely see his eyes. He gave me a small smile.

"One minute to go!"

With a few final twists, I finished tightening the screws.

"Thank you, Fish!" said the kid in the red hat.

All the other racers had started their engines. They had their hands on their wheels. They were all set to go. I raced back to my boat. I wondered how that kid knew my name.

"Welcome to the Captain Kidd Classic!" said a deep voice over the engine noise. "The first race is Class One, Eleven and Under."

All eyes moved to the judges' stand. There stood the Captain, right beside the cannon. He was wearing his fancy blue-and-gold Navy uniform, the same one he had worn when he won a Medal of Honor for bravery.

I put on the mirrored sunglasses. I opened the throttle. Then I pulled the rope to start the Seagull.

No luck.

"Fair winds and following seas!" the Captain's voice boomed through the megaphone. He pulled the rope on the cannon.

I pulled the rope on the *Fireball.*

KA-BOOM! went the cannon.

All the boats surged forward—except for the *Fireball....*

# AND Z WINNER IS . . .

I tugged hard on the rope.

VROOOOOM!

The Seagull started and the *Fireball* surged forward. The other boats were already yards away. They raced toward the bell buoy. I could hear the crowd roaring.

I had to get the *Fireball* up on plane if I ever wanted to catch up. I pulled out the throttle to full.

WHOOOOOOSH!

The *Fireball* shot forward. But the other boats were even farther away now. As I gained speed, I could see Bryce in the *Viper* in the lead. True in the *Barracuda* was next, with Max in his dad's boat, which was called the *Neutrino* (his dad is a scientist, a physicist, actually), just after him, and the *Comet* just behind. Then came three other boats. Edging up to them was the silver boat called the *Zephyr*, with the boy in the red baseball cap.

SPLASH!

Two of the boats fell off plane. The *Zephyr* passed them and the one ahead of them.

VROOM!

I zoomed past the same two boats.

PHWOMP!

## PLANING

A boat planes when it sails over its own bow wave, so that only a small section of hull (body of the boat) is in the water. This allows the boat to go faster than the maximum theoretical hull speed.

The third one suddenly slowed coming around the curve. It must have fallen off plane, too. I surged past it. Way up ahead, the *Zephyr* passed the *Comet* and then the *Barracuda*. The *Viper* was just yards in front of it. The motor on that *Zephyr* sure was fast!

The *Neutrino* slowed down. I passed it with a nod at Max. Two O in the *Comet* was about twenty yards ahead of me. An Alumacraft like the *Comet* is light, which can make it fast, but the engine on this one was an old nine horsepower.

The *Fireball* started catching up. Ten yards. Then five. Two O looked over at me as I passed and gave me a thumbs-up.

Woo-hoo! The *Fireball* was zooming faster than it ever had before. It must have been because of the racing fuel. Eli had said it could give me one or two more points of horsepower.

I could do this. I could beat Bryce. I just had to stay on plane and keep cruising.

"Go, *Fireball!*" I heard someone scream.

"Go, *Viper!*" I heard another voice yell.

Whistles and shouts filled the air. I could feel the crowd's excitement. I gripped the wheel tighter.

Next came the *Barracuda*. We edged back and forth, see-sawing for the lead, until True fell off plane and I raced ahead of him. The *Zephyr* was now less than ten yards ahead of me. It was right behind the *Viper*. The bell buoy was just up ahead.

"Go, *Fireball*, go!" I said, gripping the wheel.

I pulled back on the throttle to slow the boat slightly as I came into the turn by the buoy. I turned the wheel gently so the *Fireball* wouldn't come off plane.

THUNK!

The *Zephyr* hit the water just ahead of me.

It slowed down. It came off plane, taking the turn too fast. When I passed the boy in the red cap, he looked at me and smiled. The *Viper* was now just yards ahead.

"Get ready to get slayed!" Bryce yelled over his shoulder.

I edged up to him. The two of us raced side by side.

"You'll never pass me!" Bryce shouted, waving his fist.

I looked over at him as we raced neck and neck, our bows perfectly matched, our engines humming along at the same speed. It felt amazing to move so fast, the sun shining on the water, the crowd watching from the dock. Racing in the Classic was way better than I had ever imagined.

"Woo-hoo!" I felt so happy, I couldn't help whooping.

"Woo-hoo!" The crowd whooped back.

"Give it up, Finelli!" yelled Bryce.

POP!

The *Viper* slowed and then came to a stop.

I could see Bryce's shocked, angry face as I shot past him. I would never tell him I told him so, but I had told him his propeller was going to be a problem.

The *Fireball* was in the lead.

I could see the dock up ahead. The crowd was waving and shouting. All eyes were on me as I approached the finish line. I was going to do it. I was going to beat Bryce. I was so excited, I held my breath. The *Fireball* was about to smoke the *Viper* and win the race.

WHOOOSH!

The *Zephyr* suddenly whizzed past me and crossed the finish line first.

The boy in the red hat won the race!

The crowd cheered and yelled.

KA-BOOM! The Captain shot off the cannon.

I was in a daze as I docked the *Fireball*. The other racers pulled up to the dock and tied up their boats, too. I couldn't believe I had lost. I hopped onto the dock and tied my line to a post. I was so close. But the truth was that silver boat was super fast, that kid in the red hat was a good racer, and that brand-new Evinrude was a fast motor.

The crowd parted so that the boy in the red hat could walk up to the judges' stand. Mr. Billings had a big frown on his face, probably because Bryce had lost. For a second, I actually felt bad for Bryce. Beck had won both years he was in our division, so I was sure Bryce would be hearing all about that from his dad.

Mr. de Quincy and Mr. Blue smiled at the crowd.

"The winner of the Captain Kidd Classic, Class One, Eleven and Under Division, is the *Zephyr* and . . ." Mr. Blue frowned at his sheet. "There doesn't seem to be a name here." He looked up at the boy in the red hat.

The boy pulled off his hat. Long brown hair tumbled out. He wasn't a boy at all. He was a girl. And not just any girl.

He—I mean, *she*—was none other than Clementine de Quincy!

My mouth dropped open in surprise, but no one looked more shocked than Mr. de Quincy.

"Clementine?!"

She grinned at her father as he hugged her.

"But how?" he sputtered, staring at his daughter in shock. "You never said anything . . ."

"I figured since you care so much about boats, I would show you how much I like boats, too," said Clementine.

"But why didn't you tell me?"

"I wanted to surprise you," she said, hugging her dad. "I swore the boating instructor at the club to secrecy, and he let me use the *Zephyr*, one of his boats. See, I really was listening all those times you taught me about boats."

Mr. de Quincy slung his arm proudly around Clementine's shoulders. "You had a great race."

The crowd clapped and cheered, their eyes on the father and daughter.

"Congratulations!" Mr. Blue handed Clementine the silver cup while the crowd cheered.

"Coming in right behind for a close second was the *Fireball* and Fish Finelli!"

The crowd clapped and cheered for me. I could see Roger and T. J. jumping up and down and hooting. Not far behind them were my parents and Uncle Norman, with Feenie on his shoulders.

"Third place goes to Two O, that is Owen Osborn, in the *Comet*," finished Mr. Blue.

Two O and I slapped palms and whooped. Roger and T. J., who had pushed their way through the crowd, bumped fists with us, too, hooting all the while.

"Zee winner may be zee *Zephyr*," said Roger, buzzing his Z's loudly, "but *zee Fireball* will always be *zee* winner to me."

Just then Mr. de Quincy's voice boomed out, "Everyone is invited to a party at the Sandstone Club tonight!"

# HERE WE GO AGAIN... AGAIN!

I tugged on the collar of the white shirt my mom made me wear as we entered the Sandstone Club and headed to the party. The blue tie was choking me and my shiny loafers were pinching my toes. Feenie wore a pink, lacy dress and for once she wasn't wearing her fairy wings. My parents were all dressed up, too. My dad even had on his blue blazer with the gold buttons that he only wears on very special occasions.

"Yo, Fish!" Roger called, standing with T. J. off to the side of the very crowded ballroom.

I noticed they were both dressed up, too. They looked about as uncomfortable as I felt. The whole place was decorated pirate style. There were ropes hanging on the walls like rigging and a crow's nest all the way up on the ceiling. Waiters wearing eye patches and bandannas tied pirate style on their heads walked around with trays. Trunks with plastic gold spilling out of them were placed around the room.

"Ladies and gentlemen," said Mr. de Quincy into a microphone. "Mr. Blue would now like to officially present the silver cups to the winners." He and Mr. Blue stood side by side on a stage at the front of the room.

"Race One's winning cup has been engraved with the name of this year's winning boat," began Mr. Blue. He pointed to the trophy. "The *Zephyr*, piloted by Clementine de Quincy."

Clementine walked up to the front and he handed her the cup. There was another round of applause, but Clementine wasn't smiling.

"Wait!" she called over the noise of all the clapping. She stared out at the audience, as if she were looking for someone. Her eyes rested on me all of a sudden, and she motioned for me to come up to the stage.

"Huh?"

"Fish, that's your cue, dude." Roger elbowed me.

So Clementine *was* looking for someone. She was looking for me. My parents smiled as I passed them. Uncle Norman winked as he put his arm around Venus's shoulders.

I had almost reached the front of the room when I tripped over something. As I caught my balance, I looked up. Bryce was standing there with a nasty grin on his face. He was wearing a fancy white suit.

"Watch your step, loser," he said so low only I could hear.

"If Fish Finelli hadn't fixed my carburetor, I would never have won," said Clementine. She turned to me and grinned.

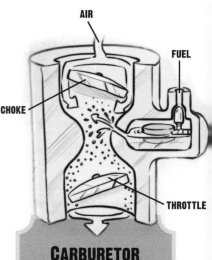

A murmur ran through the crowd. Mr. Blue looked at Mr. de Quincy in surprise, but Mr. de Quincy just smiled, as if he knew this was going to happen all along.

"And the *Fireball* might have come in first, because he wouldn't have gotten a late start. This cup really belongs to Fish."

I stood there in shock as Mr. Blue and Mr. de Quincy talked to Clementine.

## CARBURETOR

A carburetor combines air and fuel to create an internal combustion engine. It is a metal tube with a throttle (adjustable plate) that controls the amount of airflow. A narrowing in the tube (the venturi) creates a vacuum, inside of which is a hole (the jet) that allows the vacuum to pull in fuel.

Mr. Blue picked up the microphone. "As I just now found out, the *Zephyr* would not have been in the race at all if it weren't for Fish Finelli, who jeopardized his own start time in order to help a fellow mariner. He sets a fine example for all boaters."

There was more clapping and a bunch of hooting that I knew without looking had to be Roger and T. J.

Clementine handed the cup to me. "Fish and I are going to split the prize money and share the trophy. He gets it for six months, starting now."

Everyone laughed and clapped.

"No, you should have it first," I said, handing it back to her, "since the *Zephyr* really won."

She handed it to me again. "No, you!"

"And now for the winner of the second race," said Mr. Blue. "Beck Billings in the *Poseidon*."

Everyone cheered and clapped. Mr. Billings patted Beck on the back, beaming as he watched him weave his way to the podium. Mrs. Billings adjusted her long pearl necklace, a huge smile pasted across her face. Bryce looked away and his eyes met mine. His sad, sour-looking expression suddenly turned angry. I didn't care.

I couldn't stop smiling as I looked down at the trophy in my arms, thinking of Mr. Blue saying I was a fine mariner. I realized right then that it meant more to me than winning or losing.

The other winners were announced, but I barely heard as Two O came up to congratulate me. Even True gave me the thumbs-up.

Then music started playing, and the adults started dancing. Feenie and Mmm were dancing, too. Most of the kids were gathered at the other end of the room near the food. I headed toward Roger and T. J.

"You know, I really couldn't have done it without you," Clementine said, coming up beside me. "Thank you for fixing my carburetor."

"It was no big deal," I said.

"What was no big deal?" asked Roger.

"It was *so*," said Clementine, her green eyes serious.

"What was so?" asked T. J., popping a shrimp in his mouth.

"It was *so* a big deal that Fish fixed my carb, because if he hadn't, then I wouldn't have won," said Clementine. "And he might have."

I shrugged. "I don't know about that, because the *Zephyr* is a really fast boat."

Clementine smiled. "It is fast. That's why it's called the *Zephyr*. It means—"

". . . wind!" we both said and burst out laughing.

"Oh, man," said Roger. "A girl Great Brain."

Roger and T. J. started laughing, too, as a girl in a sparkly white dress danced by with True. She waved at Clementine. Summer and Beck danced by next.

"Summer and Beck sitting in a tree," crooned Roger, loud enough for Summer to hear. She stuck her tongue out at him behind Beck's back and then danced Beck away.

Next thing we knew, Two O came dancing over, waving at us as he twirled some Sandstone Club girl around so fast, I was surprised she didn't throw up.

Roger nodded toward Clementine and raised his eyebrows at me.

"What?" I mouthed.

He kicked me hard and whispered, "Ask her to dance, Great Brain!"

I blushed and felt my whole face turn red. I glanced over at Clementine, who was looking at me. I turned even redder.

"Um . . . do you want to . . . um . . ." Before I could get the words out, she was already nodding.

She reached for my arm and we headed out to the dance floor. I was so nervous, I couldn't think of a word to say. I had never danced with a girl before, unless you counted my mom. My stomach felt funny, like it was filled with jellyfish.

"Get out of my way, loser," said Bryce, taking Clementine's other arm. "I'm dancing with her."

"You are not," I said. "And just who are you calling a loser?"

Clementine looked from me to Bryce and back again. I was way too mad to say the alphabet this time. Right is right, and wrong is just plain old wrong. First Bryce tripped me, and now he was trying to take away my first-ever dance with a girl.

"You," said Bryce.

More than angry, what I realized I was feeling was brave. It might have been because of the trophy or the fact that Clementine was standing right beside me. "You're the loser," I said, staring him right in the eye. "Since I won the bet."

Kids stopped talking to listen. All eyes were on us.

"You did not," said Bryce. "You didn't really win the race."

"Clementine did," added Trippy.

"But he did win the race to Get Lost," said Roger.

"And even if I didn't come in first, you were eating my spray in the Classic, just like I said you would be," I said.

"He beat you fair and square," said Roger. "He bet you he would beat you, and he did."

Bryce turned red. "You guys think you're so hot."

"Smoking hot," said Roger.

"Guess what? You're still losers. None of you belongs at this club. You're not members and you never will be."

"Knock it off, Bryce," I said.

"Don't tell me what to do," said Bryce. He moved closer to me with an angry frown. Trippy was right behind him.

"I'm not scared of you," I said, holding my ground.

"You think you're so brave?"

I wasn't feeling all that brave anymore, with the two of them standing over me, but I was really mad. I wasn't going to let him push me or Rog or Teej around, just because his family belonged to the snooty Sandstone Club and ours didn't. "Yes."

"Prove it."

I stared around frantically trying to think of something. My eye was caught by a painting of a whale hunt on the wall next to me. "I'll go into the one-legged whaler's haunted house." I blurted out the words.

"On the night of the full moon," said Bryce.

A murmur went through the crowd. No one ever went into the haunted house, especially not at night and never on the night of the full moon when everyone who believes in ghosts says they have the most power.

"And you have to bring out the one-legged whaler's harpoon!" said Trippy. "As proof . . ."

I didn't say anything for a minute.

"You going to take the dare or not, Finelli?" asked Bryce.

Roger and T. J. looked at me. I knew they were thinking about the ghost of the one-legged whaler, who cursed anyone who dared to enter and then ran them through with his rusty harpoon and locked them in the dungeon, where they slowly turned into rotting corpses.

"I knew you were too chicken," said Bryce.

"Scaredy-cat," added Trippy.

"I'll do it," I said. "Anyway, there are no such things as ghosts."

"Guess you'll find out."

"Count me in," said Roger. He elbowed T. J. so hard a piece of dinner roll popped out of his mouth.

"Me too," said T. J.

"Here we go again . . . *again* . . ." said Roger.

There were no such things as ghosts . . . were there? It looked like it wouldn't be long before we found out. . . .

# GHOSTS DON'T
# WEAR GLASSES

## SNEAK PREVIEW
## CHAPTER

# A DATE WITH DOOM

"Once, twice, three—shoot!"

Roger and T. J. flung out their hands. Roger's was in a fist. T. J.'s was flat.

"Paper covers rock!" said T. J. "I win!"

"You went a split second after me," said Roger. "Do over."

"That's what you said the last three times," said T. J.

It was a hot Wednesday afternoon. We were on our way to the Whooping Hollow One stop with a wagon full of cans and bottles to recycle. Once we cashed them in, we were going to use the money for ice cream at Toot Sweets.

"He's right, Roger," I said. "It's your turn to pull. And quit talking. I'm trying to calculate the volume of the wagon, which is a rectangular prism, and multiply it by point oh-five to figure out how much money we're going to get."

"Fish, it's vacation, which means no more decimals. Hooray! One more time, Teej, pretty please with chocolate-chip pancakes and cheese fries on top," said Roger.

T. J. shrugged.

"And now for the Spanish version," said Roger. "Uno, dos, tres—shoot!"

"Rock smashes scissors!" said T. J. "I win—again."

Roger sighed dramatically as he grabbed the wagon handle.

"What are you going to get?" said T. J. "I'm thinking two scoops of bubble-gum ice cream with sour gummies."

"Ew, T. J.! Bubble gum is nasty with sours," said Roger. "Blueberry Bomb or Pineapple Pizazz are much better."

"Reality check, guys," I said. "That's not going to be enough money for double scoops with toppings for each of us. Those cost four dollars and fifty cents, which means we need thirteen dollars and fifty cents plus tax. If the volume of the wagon is roughly one hundred and seventy-two cubic inches, that's not—"

"Dude, we've got hundreds of bottles and cans here," said Roger as we crossed the railroad tracks onto Main Street. "Fourteen, fifteen bucks, I bet. Your turn." He thrust the wagon handle into my hand and raced ahead before I could open my mouth.

T. J. and I caught up with Roger about a block from Toot Sweets. The line was already out the door.

"Boo!" Micah and Silas King popped out from behind the mailbox between Get Whooped, the surfer shop, and Toot Sweets. They're twins a year older than we are who run a clam stand on Two Mile Harbor.

"Hey, dudes," said Roger, as we all bumped fists. "Clam business slow? Need us to help you out and find some oysters?"

We had briefly worked for the twins earlier in the summer so we could pay their older brother, Eli, to help us fix up our boat, the *Fireball*, to get it ready to race in the Captain Kidd Classic.

"My offer still stands," said Mi, flipping through a fat wad of dollar bills and counting them under his breath. "You get fifty percent of whatever you catch—oysters or clams."

"And I still say seventy-five percent is only fair," said Roger.

"It's a better get-rich-quick scheme than *that*," said Mi, tilting his head toward the wagon.

"This isn't a get-rich-quick scheme," said Roger. "We're recycling, helping to save the planet and the polar bears so their ice caps don't sink."

"You mean melt," I said. "Due to global warming caused partly by the erosion of the ozone layer as a result of our use of fossil fuels and the carbon—"

"It's summer vacation, Great Brain, please," said Roger.

"Tell me you're not in it for the money," said Mi.

I laughed. "He got you, Rog, since you're not getting a double scoop with toppings without it."

"Are you guys really going into the one-legged whaler's haunted house?" asked Si all of a sudden, pushing his glasses back up on his nose. "Even with the doorway crying blood and everything."

"What?" I said, my heart beating faster in my chest.

I had been trying to forget about my dare with Bryce Billings, the bully of Whooping Hollow Elementary who thinks he is the coolest dude ever. We're supposed to go into that house and bring out the whaler's bloody harpoon.

That's right, his bloody harpoon. It's a long story, and believe it or not I made up the dare myself. When I lose my temper, I say stuff that surprises even me.

"Burt Babinski said he saw the blood himself, dripping right down the front door," said Si.

"Hey," said T. J., pointing to the *Whooping Hollow Star* newspapers in the kiosk next to the mailbox. "Look!"

Roger read the headline aloud: "WHOOPING HOLLOW WHALER'S HOUSE FOR SALE."

"The Hannibal W. Royce house, built in 1845 by the famous one-legged whaling captain and Whooping Hollow legend, is soon to be for sale," I read.

"No wonder the house is crying blood," said T. J.

"It's not like it's true," I said. "Doors can't bleed."

"Fish has a point there, Teej," said Roger. "I mean, we're talking Burt Babinski. The same individual who claimed that he had been struck by lightning while taking a shower, which is how come he now has X-ray vision."

"So, when you going in?" asked Mi, looking up from his wad of cash.

"I don't know," I said. "We have to set the date with Bryce."

"A date with doom," said Si solemnly.

"I wouldn't want to be in your shoes," said Mi.

"Is that because you're more of a flip-flop sort of guy?" joked Roger.

"You know what I mean," said Mi. "Not that I believe in ghosts, but if I were a ghost, the one-legged whaler's house is just the kind of creepy place I'd call home."

"The legend is that the whaler's ghost stabs anyone through the heart with his bloody harpoon who dares to enter that house," said Si, blinking behind his glasses. "'Cause a killer white whale bit his leg off and he's still mad about it all these hundreds of years later."

"You mean a right whale, not a white whale," I said. "Whalers hunted right whales because they had the most blubber. That's why they were called right whales. And they weren't killers. The orca, though it's known as the killer whale—"

"Enough with the marine science, Oh Great Brainio," said Roger.

"I hope Bryce forgets about the dare," said Si. "For your sake."

## RIGHT WHALES

About 50 feet long, weighing up to 70 tons (14,000 pounds), they have hairy heads with bumpy patches of skin, small eyes, and two blowholes. Named right whales by whalers because they were the "right" whales to hunt since they were slow swimmers (averaging 6 miles per hour), making them easy to catch, and had thick blubber that could be turned into lots of oil. So few are left, they are endangered.

"Not likely," said Mi. "Since I heard his dad is the one who is trying to buy the house in the first place."

"Like I said, that explains the bleeding," said T. J., his brow furrowed. "Dr. Ghost B. Gone says that sometimes when an entity gets upset, it acts out in ways the living can see. So I bet the entity is upset that the house is being sold."

"Entity?" asked Si.

"That's what Dr. Ghost B. Gone calls ghosts," said T. J. "It's the technical name."

*Dr. Ghost B. Gone* is T. J.'s favorite TV show. It's about a crazy ghost hunter who investigates hauntings. He's also not allowed to watch it, because it's on at ten o'clock at night and it's creepy. So he sneaks behind his dad's recliner while his parents watch the show.

"It takes a really powerful entity to make a door drip blood," T. J. said. "That means this ghost is no orb or poltergeist or streak. I'm afraid to say it sounds like the work of an elemental."

"What in the heck is an elemental?" I asked. Not that I believe in ghosts or anything.

"It's *all* mental, if you ask me," said Roger, twirling his index finger around his right ear.

"No, it's not," said T. J. in the serious voice he uses with teachers and his mom. "There's lots of proof ghosts exist. An elemental is an entity that can take full physical form. Dr. Ghost B. Gone says you have to be very careful when you deal with one because an elemental can—"

"It's elementary, my dear Watson," Roger said in a fake English accent.

"An elemental can what?" asked Si, his green eyes bulging like a frog's behind his glasses.

Before T. J. could answer, the line began to move and a group of kids came out of Toot Sweets. One of them had slicked-back blond hair and was wearing a Sandstone Country Club rash guard, board shorts, and the gold-rimmed sunglasses I knew only too well. Bryce had gotten them after our first bet. He lost that bet and had to give me his mirrored sunglasses when we found Captain Kidd's treasure. I could see his trusty sidekick, Trippy, and his new best buddy, True, a boy I didn't know because he belonged to the club and only lived here in the summer.

"Incoming!" said Roger.

I looked away, hoping Bryce wouldn't see me.

"Oooh, check out the trash collectors," said Bryce with a

smirk on his face. Behind him, Trippy and True snickered. "Hey, I think I have something for you."

Bryce handed Trippy his chocolate-dip cone and pulled something out of his backpack. It was a not quite empty Gatorade bottle. Before I could make a move, he tossed it into the wagon. Blue Gatorade dripped all over the cans.

"Hey!" I said, my face burning. "Take that back."

"Why?" said Bryce. "It's garbage and you're collecting garbage, right?"

Heads turned. Bryce had that effect on people. If we were amphibians in a tropical rain forest, he'd be the bright-yellow poison dart frog, deadly and impossible to miss. I'd be a panther chameleon, changing colors to blend into the background—except for when I lose my temper and open my big mouth, that is.

"Not yours," I said, feeling my ears start burning, too, as I grabbed the Gatorade bottle. I wanted to throw it at him, but I just tossed it onto the ground by his feet.

"Sorry," said Bryce without sounding sorry at all. "I thought you could use the five cents."

Trippy and True snickered again.

"How dare you?" I began, my hands balling into fists.

"Speaking of dares, Mr. 'I'm-so-brave I'll go into the one-legged whaler's haunted house and bring out his bloody harpoon,'" said Bryce in a high-pitched voice, as if he were imitating a girl, "when are you planning to go into the house?"

More eyes turned our way.

"Any day now," I said, as Roger and T. J. glanced over at me in surprise.

SNORT. "It better be, because my dad is going to bulldoze that place soon. Unless you're too chicken . . . "

"Bawk! Bawk!" said Trippy, flapping his arms.

"Bawk! Bawk!" said True, flapping too.

"I'm not chicken," I said, my face turning an even deeper shade of red.

"You know what they say about that house?" said Bryce, dropping his voice to a loud whisper. "People go in and never come out. The whaler's ghost stabs them with his bloody harpoon right through the heart and then he puts their bodies in the basement, which is filled with the bones from all the dead people he already stabbed. Remember what happened to that paperboy who didn't know the house was haunted?"

A murmur ran through the crowd.

"He went to deliver the paper and then he was never heard from again. All they found was his bloody baseball cap. He's down there, too, in that basement, his body slowly turning into a rotting corpse."

T. J. and Roger stiffened beside me.

"That's just a story," I said, although it sure was creepy.

Just then a girl with long black hair pushed her way toward Bryce. She was wearing a wet suit and holding a vanilla ice cream cone.

"Ready to go?" she said.

"Hi, Clementine!" My face got hot again. I bet I was as red as my mom's cherry Jell-O.

"Hi, Fish!" she smiled, happy to see me.

Clementine won the Captain Kidd Classic boat race. Besides being an excellent mariner, she also happens to be just about the prettiest girl in the world. She hangs out with Bryce because his parents are friends with her dad and they live next door to each other. Even though he's nasty to me and so many other kids, he's always real nice to her.

"You mean 'Hi, chicken,'" said Bryce.

"I'm not chicken!"

"Bawk! Bawk!" All three boys flapped their arms.

A couple of kids laughed.

"Yeah," said Roger. "He's not chicken. He's going into the one-legged whaler's haunted house, just like he said."

"My father says out with the old, in with the new. He's going to put up a bunch of luxury condos with a private golf course and a spa." Bryce's father wasn't known as the real estate king for nothing. "Who cares about some old whaler, anyway? He's dead. He killed some whales. Big deal."

"I sure hope you don't get stabbed by the bloody harpoon, Finelli," called our friend, Two O, from farther up the line.

"Just admit it, loser," said Bryce. "You're afraid of the ghost, which is why you haven't gone in there. And so are your little chicken friends."

"Quit calling me a loser." All eyes were on me, including Clementine's. "I'm not scared and neither are my friends."

"Yeah," said Roger.

T. J. was madly chewing his gum, his face pale. Roger elbowed him.

"Um . . . yeah . . ."

"We've just been waiting for . . . " What, I wondered? Special equipment? Information? The right moment? That was it! The right moment. How had I forgotten? Although it looked like Bryce had forgotten, too.

"Guts? Since you obviously don't have any," said Bryce, high-fiving Trippy.

"We've got plenty of guts," I said, gritting my teeth. "We've just been waiting for the full moon like you dared me, remember? It was your idea."

"Yup," said Roger.

"So, the night of the full moon is when we're going in."

"Right," sneered Bryce. "You're all talk, chicken!"

"I am NOT." How dare Bryce call me a liar? I was about to boil over, like molten lava out of a volcano.

"I think Saturday night is a full moon," said Clementine. "I bet that's when Fish was planning to go into the whaler's house. Weren't you, Fish?"

I nodded. Saturday night was the night of the full moon. Uncle Norman asked my dad to go midnight fishing for stripers then. He always says the full moon is the best time to catch them.

"So, Saturday night it is. We'll meet you at the one-legged whaler's at eight o'clock." I glared at Bryce.

"Just before moonrise," said Roger.

"Be there, or everyone will know the truth," said Bryce, taking a bite of his cone. He stalked off before I could say another word.

"BAWK! BAWK!" Trippy and True flapped their arms, laughing as they headed after him.

Clementine gave me a thumbs-up before she followed.

"Good luck on your date with doom!" said Mi.

"You're going to need it . . . " added Si.